I0734445

By R. L. Clayton

*Sea Species*
*The Envoy*
*Genesis*
*Wings of the WASP*

Visit R. L. Clayton's website
www.evolutionriver.com

R. L. Clayton

# DEAD & DEAD FOR REAL

For my sister, Col. Sharon Clayton Volgyi, USA, who will never get the chance to read this book. You would like it. It was only after it was too late to talk to you that I learned how special you were to so many others. You would never tell me.

This book started as a dream. Many of my story ideas begin that way. The *Tall Grass Editing CoOp* helped me develop the dream into a novel. My special thanks to the members. My friend and mentor, Alexis Powers, continues to inspire my writing. Her Oro Valley Writers Motivational Workshop has helped many authors to publish, and opened the community of writers to me. What fun these people are!

A special thanks to my graphic artist, Steve Linebaugh, for the book covers, posters, newsletters, and artwork. Without him, I would be just a name writing words on a page.

Thank you all.

# DEAD & DEAD FOR REAL

# PROLOGUE

Officer Mario Cava walked down Congress Street away from the Joel Valdez Bus Terminal. This late at night, it was deserted – almost. In the shadow behind a car ahead, he saw a crouched figure intent on something further down the street. Something was wrong here, he thought. With his hand on his gun, he approached the man, whose back as to him.

"You. Freeze! On your knees! Cross your legs behind you, raise you hands over your head." The man complied. Mario approached, ready to draw his weapon at the slightest wrong move. "With your left hand, give me your ID."

A gravelly voice said, "Officer, move slowly. Place your right hand on your heart and look down."

It was a command, from someone used to giving orders. Mario eased his hand to his chest. A red dot appeared. Jesus! It was a laser sight! He was targeted!

"Now you be real quiet and listen to me. I know you're wearing body armor good for handguns, but behind that sight is an M1-A, and the .308 bullet will blow your heart out the back of your chest. Let's keep this slow and easy. What's your name?"

"Cava," Mario answered. He was rattled.

"Keep acting like you're rousting me, but ease behind this car so it's between you and that van ahead."

Mario looked at a white van parked at the curb two cars ahead. "Who are you?"

Ignoring the question, the voice rasped out, "Use your shoulder mic as if you're calling me in, but radio 'Officer needs backup.' Tell them to hold a perimeter, come in silent, and await your order to block off the street ahead and behind."

What was going on, thought Mario? Minutes dragged by. Just as he was about to ask, the silence of the street was broken by loud thumping music rocking the van. He looked at it and then down to the kneeling man. His radio crackled. The cars were in place.

Through the beat of the music he heard the gravely voice again. "Those guys want you to go up to their car to tell them to turn it down. Then they'll blow your head off. Tell the squad cars to move in, block off the intersections, full lights and sirens. Get down behind this car."

The wails of the sirens caused eerie reverberations as flashing lights of red and blue strobed across the buildings. The van's engine roared and the back doors flew open. As Mario ducked, the staccato reverberation of a machinegun echoed. Glass showered around him, and the car rattled as bullets struck it. The van took off with squealing tires. There was a thunderous boom, and it slued, hitting a parked car and rolling onto its side. Sparks flew as it slid along the street. A figure crawled from the back. Another boom sounded, and his head disappeared in a red mist.

Mario turned to ask what happened, but he was alone. A small card lay on the sidewalk. Pulsing red and blue from the lights, he read it. "Congratulations, Officer Cava. You just solved the cop killing last week in Albuquerque. Gotta go. I have more work to do."

# Chapter 1

Nick sprinted down the deserted alley, the ululating sound of the sirens chasing him as it echoed off the buildings. He skidded around a corner and jumped into the van idling at the curb.

"Hit it, Kiki. East to Fourth, south to $22^{nd}$ St. We'll get on I-10 going north."

The petite woman behind the wheel pressed the accelerator, careful not to speed. Entering the light flow of traffic on Interstate 10, they became another westbound car.

As they passed downtown Tucson, red and blue lights winked at them between the buildings. A helicopter circled the tall buildings, a bright beam stabbing the night, spotlighting the ground, seeking them.

"Nice shooting, Kiki." Nick's grin was hidden in the dark. Her talent as a sniper still amazed him.

She pushed the strands of brown hair from her eyes. A grim smile showed in the glow of the dash lights. "Two hundred meters, piece of cake.

Most of the work I did in Afghanistan was five to eight hundred meters."

Nick turned to face her. "Ricardo had that ambush right. He has a lot more information we need. Could be a long night prying it out of him."

"Yeah. Last night was a late enough for me."

Kiki changed the subject, trying to lighten the mood. "I thought that cop was going to cuff you. That would have made things a bit dicey." She chuckled at the vision of Nick running with his hands behind his back.

"The dot on his chest was effective. He was much more willing to listen after seeing that."

The city became a glow in the sky behind them. Ahead loomed the shadowy spike of Picacho Peak. The sign for the Dairy Queen was a beacon for their exit. Easing into the Picacho Peak RV resort, few of the units showed lights.

This RV park was popular with the nomadic caravan crowd. Away from the city, the views of the mountains and the desert valley were spectacular. Night skies were crystal clear, the stars brilliant pin-pricks of light.

Their elderly neighbors would sit outside and chat RV talk or tell tales of past lives. This late though, all seemed to be soundly asleep. Kiki eased through the bus-sized motorhomes not wanting to disturb them. She backed the van into the slot beside their twenty-nine foot motorhome and turned it off.

In the silence, she softly said, "Nick, I'll unload the car, you check on Ricardo." Easing the door shut, Kiki surveyed their area again. It was quiet.

Mounting the steps, Nick glanced around. The outside light had been left on, as was a small light above the stove. The door opened noiselessly as he checked inside. Nothing was amiss. It was as they had left it. He turned the outside light off.

Both his and Kiki's actions were those born from the caution of conflict. Being surprised could be lethal.

Leaning through the van's sliding door, Kiki cased her semi-automatic version of the M-14 rifle, removing the night-vision scope. It went into its own padded case. With her hand on her holstered Berretta, she glanced around again. No lights, no eyes. She imagined the oldsters snoring away. If they only knew.

Hoisting the cases on her shoulder, she eased the van door closed and mounted the steps in the darkness. She too glanced around the interior. It was neatly kept, the overhead bed in the front made to military specs, the stove wiped clean, the sink empty. Her 'tell,' the delicately balanced folded paper on the table, was as she'd left it.

The cases were stowed under the bench seats. She turned toward the rear of the RV. The back room, once a bedroom, now resembled a hospital room. The large rear window and the side window were blacked out. Electrical monitors were mounted on the walls, but the dominating feature was the large box in the center of the floor. It resembled a rounded casket, but double the width and height. Its black plastic surface absorbed all light, yet seemed to radiate in the dim room. Small lights on the side indicated it was powered. Tubes and wires ran from it to the monitors on the wall and a drip IV bag.

It was hushed, circulating fans and pumps whispering. Monitors beeped softly as they traced jagged lines while numbers indicated the conditions inside the black chamber. A flat screen monitor on the wall, the main source of light, bathed the room in its green glow. It showed a man inside the capsule, suspended in liquid. His eyes were closed, chest rising in slow rhythm as he breathed.

The sensory deprivation chamber isolated the man from the world. He couldn't see, feel, hear, taste, or touch. Without his senses, he was a mind floating in a vast blackness.

Nick studied the green and yellow lines skipping across the monitors telling him the victim's temperature, pulse rate, respiration, blood pressure, and brainwave function. "Look through the stuff from his pockets again. See if we missed anything." he said over his shoulder.

Kiki held up the baggie. "A thousand dollars, must be a drug dealer. Nothing else unusual, drivers license, iPod, and keys. The crucifix was a help. At least we knew he was religious. Coupled with the lack of stuff in his motel room, he was ordinary, with a wad of cash. How's he doing?" asked Kiki, nodding at the chamber. "There was nothing to miss." She eased into a padded chair, one of two, the only other pieces of furniture in the room.

Glancing at the brainwave monitor, Nick said, "Sleeping and dreaming like a baby." In the other chair, he pulled a laptop computer in front of him. Tapping on a few keys, the screen showed a bar graph array with titles and numbers below. He tapped again. The bar above the word "Seds" decreased and the numbers for "cc's/hr" decreased. A few more keystrokes, and the bar above "Paraly" crept up. The one for "Adrin" also crept up.

"Time for a nightmare," Nick said.

The monitors showed increased brainwave activity, respiration, and pulse rate.

"He's waking but doesn't know where he is. Let's start." Nick put a small microphone on his shirt and turned it on.

On the flat screen, the figure jerked slightly, regaining consciousness. Nick bumped the paralytic drug, curarine, up. He had to be careful not to paralyze the diaphragm and suffocate Ricardo, but his arms and legs must be immobilized.

"Is anyone there?" asked Ricardo. In the chamber, the sound suppression system damped out his voice. He spoke, but his ears heard nothing. "Why you not answer me?"

Nick watched the respiration rate and heart rate rise. Brainwave function increased. He turned the mic off. "He's starting to panic. We'll let him."

Blood pressure and heart rate spiked. Ricardo screamed questions into a black vacuum. Nick backed the adrenalin off and increased the anti-anxiety. If Ricardo had been free of the drug-induced paralysis, he would be thrashing wildly. After several minutes, his brainwaves showed he was calming. Nick turned on the mic.

*"Ricardo de Silva,"* he said. *"I am the Lord, your God."*

Spikes of panic again rose, but not as high as before. The words Nick spoke were conducted to a bone microphone, bypassing Ricardo's ears.

*"You stand before me in judgment. Confess your life to me so your sins may be forgiven, and you are ready for the next life."*

Inside the chamber, Ricardo's moan went unheard by his ears. His eyes flicked from side to side, seeking light, but seeing only blackness.

"I am dead?" he asked of the darkness.

*"You are with me. You have left your Earthly world behind."*

Nick watched the monitors closely. He had to maintain a delicate balance to keep Ricardo immobilized yet breathing, sedated yet aware.

*"Tell me your life story. Start yesterday."*

"If you are God, you know my life."

*"I do, but you must confess to be forgiven. Things not confessed cannot be forgiven. They are a mark on your soul. You cannot enter Heaven."*

"Okay, I was at the Walmart getting food. In my car, a mask went over my head. I don't remember nothing."

*"You told me why you are here. Tell me again."*

"We had a contract to kill this cop."

*"Who is 'we'?"*

"Little Pepe and Griego, they are going to do it. I don't kill him, I don't sin."

*"Do not evade! Tell me your sins. You must leave nothing out."*

Carefully, Nick led him through his life step by step, day by day, the recording system missing nothing. The prodding went on for hours, eliciting the gruesome stories of Ricardo's thirty years, a short life.

He had gone from drug hopper to hit man before the age of fifteen. Even as he confessed, he showed no empathy for his victims, no regret for his actions. At age twenty, he was now a capitán, second in command in his brother's gang.

Kiki yawned, drained from the images elicited by the confession, by the activities of the day, by her hatred of Ricardo. She couldn't stay longer. She struggled from the chair, moving toward the front of the RV. Her head ached, her arms were heavy. She removed her boots. Too weary to do more, she climbed into the overhead bed, fully clothed in her urban cammies. She'd listen to the tapes tomorrow. Her dreams were also of violence and death.

# Chapter 2

Nick watched the sound canceling monitor. It recorded the voice, but canceled out the sound inside the sensory deprivation chamber. Nick spoke,

*"Continue with your story, Ricardo. Tell me of the killings you did."*

Ricardo's ears heard nothing, but the voice vibrated against his skull.

"If you're God, you know what happened."

*"I must hear you tell it. In the telling, I look for remorse for your sins. Without that, there can be no forgiveness."*

"Two months ago we killed those ranchers near Red Rock. There was an old man and old lady. That old man, he was tough. He lasted for hours. The old lady had a heart attack or something. We hardly touched her. The young guy, he tried to protect the kid. He tackled me, so I made him watch when we killed the kid, then we killed him, slow. We cut the heads from all of them and left them in the freezer. They had some good steaks there, so we stayed for a couple of days."

*"You felt no remorse killing the child?"*

"Oh yeah. Claro. Of course I did. She was just a little niña. We just did it because we were told to."

*"Where did you go from there?"*

"We went back home, to Albuquerque. Then the word came to kill those pendájo cops in Albuquerque. We did Tucson first so it wouldn't be so obvious we was Los Hijos, you know, Hijos de Hades, my brother's gang. Same thing with the heads. I don't care about the heads, but it was what La Sombra told us to do.

"The contract sent us back to Tucson to kill this cabrón cop. Pepe and Griego are doing that tonight."

Nick realized that Ricardo had lost track of time completely. Good.

"Tomorrow we go to El Paso to kill this woman and her two kids. It's the same orders from La Sombra. La Sombra orders us to do these things.

"While we're in El Paso, we pick up a package from Juarez. We deliver it to my brother, Joaquin, in Albuquerque."

*"What do you feel for those you kill?"*

"I feel nothing. I'm just doing my job, you know. It's just business."

*"Who is La Sombra? Tell me of the instructions you get from him."*

"This man, he gives us a list of the names and places. It has addresses where they live and work. He is not Latino or gringo. The English he speaks has an accent, you know, like from England. He drives from Phoenix with the list and money. I know because his car is from Phoenix. It says so on the license plate. I have good memory. The number is ISNO 8592."

*"What happens after a job? What do you feel?"*

"When we finish the job, my jeffe, my brother, Joaquin, calls La Sombra. He comes with the next list and more money for expenses. For our work, Hijos de Hades in Mexico pays us in powder. We sell it."

*"Do you think about the names on the list, the people you are going to kill?"*

"Nah. It's just business. We are narcotrafficantes. This job just came along, como se dice, a sideline."

*"Do you like it?"*

"I don't know. I must think 'bout that."

Nick continued with more questions, learning about Hijos de Hades, their Mexican connection.

He was exhausted and adjusted the IV, watching the monitors. Ricardo's breathing and pulse slowed. He went to sleep.

In two hours, the sun would come up. He needed to catch a few Z's. He slid into bed beside Kiki. She stirred as he spooned, his arm going around her. His breathing and hers slowed in harmony.

# Chapter 3

Kiki was dreaming, and she knew it. It made no difference; she was back in the "Sandbox" trying to recapture towns in northern Afghanistan lost six months earlier.

In classic strategy, she and her spotters had moved into town under cover of dark last night ahead of her unit to recon and set up for the attack. Many of the buildings were heavily damaged, abandoned. Through shell holes in the meter high wall around the rooftop observation point, she had a clear field down the main street of the town. The main government headquarters was at the end of that street, seven-hundred meters away. Her two spotters were at the far corners of the building, giving them views of the adjacent streets.

She'd never get used to the smell of these towns. The sewer systems were primitive where they existed. The day had been uneventful, people going about their business. Her team had set up shades camouflaged like the roof to protect them from the vicious sun, giving them a modicum of relief from the heat. Other than the government building and the mosque, they were the highest building around, so their discovery was a remote chance, until things got active. Dusk was upon them, the sun behind her.

"Got action here," said Corporal Dyson. "We got armed men in the alley entering the back of the buildings facing the main street. They're setting up to ambush our guys as they go to the plaza and the government center."

"Ditto that," said Corporal Ling. "They're setting up on this side of the street too."

Kiki radioed back to her C.O. "Captain Sabino, I suggest you split your forces and approach on the two alleys adjacent to the main street. The ragheads are setting it up as a killing zone. Let's make it one for them. Attack the ambushers from the rear and force them into the main street. I'll take what I can."

"K, we could set up at the end of the block and catch them too."

"Captain, I suspect that their escape route is through the civilians at the end of the street. If you fire up the street, they'll be in the background. If you begin your attack at the far end, it'll block that avenue."

"Roger that, 'K'. I got four guys securing your back. Don't shoot them."

"Keep them off the roof." Kiki closed her channel to the captain.

"Ling, Dyson, sing out when our guys are poised to clear the buildings. Watch for civilians. The baddies are herding them out onto the street and toward the government center."

"Roger that. Are they trying to get them out of the way?" asked Dyson.

"Either that or their escape route lies through that government building and the civilians. They know we wouldn't attack it outright."

Through her peek hole, Kiki saw the street begin to clear as the people entered the plaza at the end. All was still. She checked her gear, took a drink from her hydro-pak.

"Drink up guys. When the action starts you won't have time."

The range to the plaza was seven-hundred meters, no wind, easy shots for her. Knowing the setup from drone recon, she'd opted for her M-14 over the Model 700. On semi-auto, it gave her greater firepower. The extended range of the Model 700 wasn't needed. Next to her knee was her stack of twenty round mags of .308 match ammo. Ten meters to each side at adjacent holes in the wall were other stacks.

As darkness fell, her team donned the night vision optics. Kiki liked night fighting. Her efficiency wasn't affected, but the enemy's certainly was. With her suppressor and special flash hider, her rifle was cumbersome, but the only people seeing the flash of her shot were at the other end of the bullet. Too bad for them.

"Our guys are moving in," radioed Corporal Ling.

"Here too," echoed Dyson

In the streets below silent figures crept along the building walls until they were arrayed down the alleys, three at each door.

"Setting charges now," said Ling.

Kiki tensed, breathed out and took control, becoming icy. The back doors to the buildings lining the main street nearest the plaza blew first, rattling her stack of mags, raising dust below. Strobe flashes and the staccato rattle of automatic weapons filled the night.

In the green daylight of the NV, a figure ran from one door. Kiki tracked him, pulled the trigger. Down. Another man emerged, then another from a different door. She took the first one, then the second. A head peeked around a corner, seeking her position, then ducked back. She counted one, two, and fired at the place the head had appeared. Her bullet and the head met in a red explosion. Kiki was a machine – aim, shoot, new target, aim, shoot.

Mag empty, another slid into the well smoothly. Her total focus was on the street below.

"Guys on the roof of that apartment! You need help?" asked Corporal Ling.

Only Kiki's weapon had the suppressor. If either of her spotters fired, it would give away their position. She moved to the adjacent peek hole, spotted the two men searching for her. One took cover behind some laundry; the other was in the open. She took out the sheltered one first, firing through the cloth, and swung the sight to the other. Within the cone of view, he'd seen her muzzle flash and was bringing his rifle up. It never made it to his shoulder. He went down. The rooftop was clear.

"K, are you there?"

"Yeah, Cap. Street's quiet."

"Looks like we're secure. Holy shit! Nice job in the street."

"There's two more on the roof," said Dyson.

Kiki took out the first one while he was seeking cover. The second turned to flee. He never made the door.

"K, we're moving into the main government building."

"Cap, let me scope it first. Not seeing any movement. Check the apartment building."

"Thanks. Sergeant, let's clear that structure and set up our CP. Secure the perimeter."

"Roger that, sir."

Below Kiki, her men started moving down all three streets toward the plaza. She watched only the buildings ahead of them. There was a flutter at one window. An AK! She fired, the figure dropped. The top of the government building was higher than hers, a perfect sniper site, one she would choose.

"Ling, Dyson, scope the roof of the main building. Look especially hard at the shell holes in the walls."

A bullet smacked the wall in front of Kiki. "Someone's got us."

"Saw a flash at the corner of the government building. You want I should shoot?" asked Dyson.

"Only if I don't get there first." Kiki quickly moved left to Dyson's peek hole.

She saw it. This guy was good. He was set up far enough back that she had not seen him from her central position. Only the tip of his barrel was visible. She longed for the Barrett 50. With that, she'd simply blast through the wall and take him out.

"Cap, hole near the left corner top of the government building. I don't have a shot."

"Cover, Sergeant! Put some rounds in that hole." The wall erupted around the hole as it was targeted.

That'll drive him back, Kiki thought. He knows he's been spotted. He'll set up somewhere else. "Ling, Dyson, watch for him." She darted to the right hand corner of the building. Through Ling's peek hole, she trained the crosshairs on another hole. At seven-hundred meters, the drop of the bullet would make this a tough shot. She exhaled and waited. Was she wrong? Had he fled? Ah! Movement. Her total focus was on that twelve-inch hole. A rifle barrel showed. As soon as the head was visible, she fired.

In the half second the bullet flew, she saw the face. But it wasn't a face. It was a head shrouded in a burkha. Then it was replaced by a cloud.

"Nice shooting, Sarge," said Ling.

"Thanks. She won't bother anyone else."

"She?" asked Dyson.

"Either a she or a he in she's clothing. We'll find out."

"Good one, K," guffawed Ling.

"Kiki, wake up!"

The scene blinked out. "Wha?" she mumbled.

"You were laughing in your sleep. It was scary," said Nick. He rubbed the grit from his eyes. "Besides, we need to go to Albuquerque, via El Paso. Help me hitch the van. I'll drive, you fix breakfast."

"Woman's work?" she laughed.

"Nah, while you're doing that, listen to Ricardo's tape. You need to know what's ahead."

# Chapter 4

Tucson Police Officer Mario Cava handed his report to Lieutenant Hernandez before passing copies to the others at the meeting. Looking around the conference room, he squirmed in his seat in the silence as they read. The whiteboard on the wall behind him held little information. He had rarely been in the glass-sided "fishbowl" conference room. The blinds were drawn on the windows facing the main bay, which always created curiosity in those at the desks outside. The other windows looked out over downtown Tucson.

Cava's head was fuzzy from lack of sleep. When he was on graveyard shift, he slept during the morning, but instead, he was in this meeting. Other eyes around the table were red rimmed too.

Lieutenant Hernandez stood to address the group. His five-foot eight-inch frame filled out his uniform. "Last night's shooting could have been a tragedy for us. The evidence points to a failed cop killing. It wasn't because of us that Sergeant Cava is alive. Our units on site ended up as witnesses.

"Officer Cava, you don't have much of a description of this guy." Hernandez stared at Cava, as if accusing him of negligence.

Mario looked at the table. "No sir. It was an unlit area. His ball cap was low, he kept his head down. His clothes were dark, not black but patterned, like urban cammies. He wore boots, like military issue. I'd say he was ex-military. I never saw him stand, so height and weight are hard to estimate."

Hernandez looked at the others. "The van driver and the shooter both had heavy caliber hits to the head. We're trying to find bullet fragments to confirm the description of an M1-A pointed at Officer Cava.

"Both perps had fake ID's, and the van was stolen in Albuquerque last week. Stolen tags too. Trash, road food wrappers, and cigarette butts littered the inside. There was also a Juarez newspaper. We're running prints and DNA now.

"Detective Smith, anything from the card left by our man on the sidewalk?"

"It's a standard index card. Nothing there. Writing was in felt tip. Nothing distinctive in the handwriting, but we're doing a search. We may be able to get DNA, but there was a waxy residue.

He could have coated his hands to prevent leaving anything." Frustration showed on Smith's face.

Hernandez looked at Corporal Angela Klein, the records officer. "What about his reference to the cop killing in Albuquerque?"

The petite blonde picked up a printout. "Last Friday in a northwest Albuquerque barrio, two cops were ambushed after answering a domestic dispute call. The caller claimed to be a neighbor, but that was false. When the patrol car pulled into the driveway, it was riddled. The weapons were heavy caliber. Their body armor was useless. Their weapons are missing. No casings in the car indicate they never fired a shot. Both officers were beheaded post mortem, their heads left on the hood of the patrol car." She looked up from her report. Her moist eyes glistened. In a trembling voice, she continued.

"Both officers were five-year APD veterans. Officer Ortiz was unmarried, a Marine vet from the Afghanistan war. His sister is a med-evac pilot in Saudi Arabia. She's on her way back for the services.

"Officer Mitchel was in his third year of pre-law at UNM. He joined the Albuquerque Police Department while in school, working full-time and taking classes on the side. He was married and left behind a wife and three young kids. His sister is Navy, assigned to the USS Carl Vinson. She flew in yesterday."

Klein tapped the reports on the table. "The APD has no leads at this time. None of the neighbors saw or heard anything. The area is in an old barrio. The shooters policed their brass or had catchers on the guns. There is little evidence at the scene. It may be too early to say this, but with this attack, a pattern may be developing."

Officer Cava interrupted. "You mean military ties?"

Klein nodded.

Lieutenant Hernandez frowned. "I'm going to give a friend of mine, Freddy Foster, at the FBI a call. We at least need to make them aware of this. I don't believe in coincidence, and if it is interstate, they have to come in.

"Cava, whoever this guy was, he probably saved your life. His statement 'I have more work to do' indicates he knows there will be more attempts. We may have a vigilante team. As much as I applaud what they did, we can't have them running around killing people, even if they're bad people."

He looked at the faces around the table. "Sergeant Price, I want Detective Smith to look into this guy. See if there are other instances like this. Put a profile together.

"I also want you to start checking into the shooter. Whoever was behind that trigger, had skill. Start looking at who could make those shots. The military angle may be a lead.

"Let's bring in another detective on the perps. Detective Wong, start in Albuquerque while the evidence team works the vehicle. Call in tomorrow at 3:30 for the status meeting.

"Klein, search for similar MOs of attacks on cops.

"Let's get going people."

Everybody filed out of the conference room. Hernandez went to his office, closed the door and called Freddy. The answering machine picked up.

"No one is available to take your call. Please leave a message after the beep," said the recorded voice.

"Freddy, it's Rob Hernandez. Give me a call."

A sleepy "Hello" interrupted.

"Sleeping in, are you?"

"I was on surveillance 'til five this morning. This better be good."

Hernandez filled her in. "Do you have any active reports about attacks on ex-military or relatives of military?"

"I'll look into it. Let me call you from my office later."

# Chapter 5

Joaquin de Silva jabbed 'END' on his phone angrily. He looked around his office. Pictures of nude girls were tacked on the cheap paneling, chipped paint on the desk showed the metal beneath. The thump of bump-and-grind music from the 'showroom' filled the air. He threw his coffee cup across the room, smashing it against the wall.

What happened to Ricardo and his guys in Tucson? Yesterday, they had located their target, planned to hit him last night. No call from Ricardo this morning worried him. Calls to Ricardo went to voicemail. More worry. The phone rang. Eagerly, he looked at it, a blocked number, not Ricardo. "Hello."

"Is it done?" asked the chillingly soft voice.

"I don't know. I haven't heard from my guys. They could be on the road or it went late, and they're still holed up in the hotel, or they could be at a restaurant or…"

"I'll call back in an hour."

The phone went dead. Joaquin's handsome face contorted in fear. He had to pee. In his private bathroom, he looked in the mirror. His normally neat black hair was messy from running his hands through it. Black eyes stared back.

He called his boss in Juarez. "Hola, Juan." The conversation was in Spanish. "Ricardo hasn't called me yet."

"He called from Tucson. He'll be here tonight to pick up the package."

"Gracias."

Cautiously, Joaquin allowed himself a feeling of relief. Good. Ricardo had never picked up the payment package in Juarez before. Joaquin had decided to let Ricardo do the next hit in El Paso and pick up the package. Joaquin wouldn't have to make the trip. But why hadn't Ricardo called him? He speed-dialed Ricardo again. Straight to voicemail. Something wasn't right.

Wait until that pendájo comes back, he muttered to himself. He'd chew his ass good. Now he had to think of something to tell La Sombra when he called back.

Joaquin shivered. La Sombra was one of the few people that scared him shitless, beside his boss, Juan. At least with his boss, he had a name and telephone number. He could call and talk to him.

La Sombra called him from a number that was blocked. He did give Joaquin a contact number, but the calls were never longer than one minute. Joaquin had given him the name La Sombra, (*the shadow*). Whoever he was with, they paid well in heroin for the services, and it was always pure.

Joaquin smiled to himself. If Ricardo were on the way to El Paso, then things must have gone well in Tucson. Why hadn't he called? Joaquin headed for the bar.

The 'showroom' was the same as in any titty bar anywhere in the world. The bass of the music vibrated the walls of the dim room as the spotlighted girls wiggled across the stage, tempting dollars from the patrons. There weren't many customers at this hour of the morning, mostly swing and graveyard shift workers.

Joaquin looked at the girls. This crew of morning girls was far from the primo group who would be there tonight. He shrugged. All of them worked for tips, so it cost little to open in the mornings. The bar turned a blind eye to the extra money the girls made in the sex trade.

The drug trade was the real money anyway. Until a few months ago that was pot and meth. Now they had smack to sell. The high quality allowed them to step on it three or four times and still keep customers happy.

As he eased his five-foot-seven frame onto the bar stool, Marne gave him an egg burrito and coffee laced with Kahlua. She set a dish of fresh salsa on the bar.

"Already you know me," he said to her. Marne had only been working for him two weeks. "Nice top," he smiled at her. She also knew his tastes. The mesh top showed her breasts and jean cutoffs showed cheeks.

"Thank you, Mr. De Silva." She smiled, white teeth glowing in the black-light of the bar.

Joaquin smiled back. Her ID said she was twenty-one, but she was barely over sixteen. Joaquin knew she was ditching high school to work here. She wasn't the first.

To keep from drawing attention, he had a deal with Charon's Children, another gang in Salt Lake City, to rotate girls every three weeks. It kept the faces fresh and the patrons from getting close or asking questions. CC kept the girls for three weeks and shipped them somewhere else. Except for Marne. He watched her fill a drink order. He was going to keep her here for a while. She'd do anything he wanted for her next fix.

Jenny patted him on the back. "Morning, boss."

"Hey, Jen." She was one of the long-term girls who'd been with him for several years. Some patrons liked familiar faces. They were older girls, older patrons.

Pot legalization was on the horizon. Joaquin was setting up front stores for that. The money he was getting from selling the smack from La Sombra would fund the 'almost' legitimate business. 'Almost' because alongside the cultivated American pot, he'd be selling Mexican pot and keeping the taxes for himself.

He was going to need people he could trust, and Ricardo was putting himself in jeopardy for that position right now. Joaquin shook his head. Brother or not, he must be trustworthy. He tried calling again. It was ringing! He answered.

"Hola."

"Ricardo, what's going on? Why didn't you call me, cabrón?"

The connection was terrible. It was breaking up so badly he only understood every fourth word. It wasn't Ricardo's voice.

"Ricardo____ducha."

The phone went dead. In the shower! He hit redial. Voicemail! That asshole Ricardo better call. Joaquin got the brains and the looks in the family, Ricardo got the size. Joaquin always wanted to be taller.

# Chapter 6

The empty countryside of southeastern Arizona and western New Mexico rolled by. Nick had caught a few z's while Kiki drove. They'd been going for four hours. It was time for a break. "Kiki, let's stop in Deming for a while. We both need the rest, and we need to get rid of our 'passenger'." Nick nodded toward the back of the motorhome.

Kiki flipped on the blinker, slowing for the exit. At the stoplight, she turned south, following an arrow on a rusted sign for an RV park. Within minutes, they reached the edge of town, and a deserted RV park. The sign on the gate said "Closed for the Season," but it looked like that season was year around. Perfect. Nick picked the gate lock, and they parked at the far end, out of sight from the road. They were alone and the silence was welcome. It was nice to sit for a few minutes, cold sodas on the table in front of them.

Nick picked up Ricardo's phone and dialed the Tucson Police Department.

"May I speak to Officer Cava, please?" Nick asked.

"I'll connect you to his extension." There was a click, and the extension rang.

*"This is Officer Mario Cava. I can't take your call right now, but if you leave a message with your name and number, I'll call you back."*

It was what Nick expected. Cava was on graveyard shift. He should be home asleep now.

"Officer Cava, this is the gent you met last night. I'll call you at this extension in two hours. I have information for you."

"Not there?" asked Kiki.

"I didn't expect him to be.

"K, we're going to get whatever we can from Ricardo and..." Nick shrugged. "We have no POW facilities."

Kiki stared at the isolation chamber. Ricardo had described the murders of her family on the tape. Tears formed in her eyes, but her face hardened, her jaw clenched. This was hatred at the basest level. Nick hadn't seen this from her before.

"K, what's wrong?"

She said nothing for a while.

"Nick, I want to wake him up and take him out of the chamber conscious."

Her voice was different – hard and hollow.

"You want to kill him yourself?"

"Oh, worse than that. I want him to realize he's not dead. I want him to know he's betrayed everyone and everything he's known. I want him to realize his 'God' betrayed him. I want him to see the gates of hell open to receive him. And I want to push him through them."

Nick's mind recoiled at the vehemence in her voice. This was not the Kiki who was cool under fire, in control of herself, methodically carrying out her job. Sure, she was a killing machine, but hatred was never involved. Until now. This was personal. Her body was a statue, her clenched fists at her sides. This Kiki was a stranger to him. He imagined he saw steam rising from her head.

Kiki had never been vengeful. This was beyond torture. Their isolation chamber bypassed physical pain and entered Ricardo's mind directly. There was no return to life after what they did. Waking up would tear Ricardo's psyche apart. His belief in God would be destroyed, his grasp of reality annihilated. Killing him would be a blessing. To blow him apart this way was evil.

"K, I can't do that. It's wrong. This isn't you talking."

She shook her head, her eyes cleared. "You're right, Nick. I don't know where that came from. Do him in the chamber."

Nick brought Ricardo out of his slumber. He wasn't in good shape, too long under sedative, and their isolation chamber had scrambled his mind.

With effort, they got the directions to Joaquin's headquarters and house in Albuquerque. Ricardo had nothing else to offer. Nick felt a twinge of pity as he injected air into the IV and watched the monitors. When the traces were flat, he drained the liquid. They opened the chamber. Ricardo looked like he was asleep. Nick and Kiki lifted him out.

Kiki looked at the still form. "A part of me would like to have had him suffer like my family did, but that's revenge."

She shook her head once. "We have others to work on." Kiki stared at his closed eyes and slack mouth. They dried him off and dressed him in shabby clothes from Goodwill.

From the State Highway 71 to Columbus, the van turned onto a dirt trail. There was nothing in sight for miles. The road probably went to a rancher's stock tank, but the land was empty. They could dump him here, get some rest and make El Paso by this evening.

"This country reminds me of the Sandbox," said Kiki. She wanted conversation to move her thoughts away from the experience in the motorhome. The emotions that had taken over her were worrisome. A black cloud of hatred had risen within her, obscuring her reason. It was understandable, but she was better than that.

"Yeah, me too. I saw most of it from the air. That just gave me a bigger view of nothing." He laughed. Kiki joined him, her laughter noticeably forced.

At a non-descript wash, they removed the body and pushed it under a bush with an empty water bottle. They wiped their footprints away and their tire prints for two hundred yards up the road. Now he was just another hapless illegal migrant trying to cross. Too bad. The coyotes would age him and the buzzards would draw attention, eventually. Or not.

Neither spoke on the drive back to the motorhome.

In the motorhome, they both lay down for a short nap. Last night had been long. Nick rolled over and kissed Kiki on the cheek. "We did good. Got your family's killers and enough information to go after the others."

Kiki kissed him back, not on the cheek. "I need this." She reached below his waist. Their lovemaking was not hurried, but certainly not leisurely. After the release, both fell into exhausted sleep.

Nick woke first. It was midafternoon. Time to get moving to El Paso for the meeting. And he needed to call Officer Cava back. He let Kiki sleep.

Mario sounded pissed. "It's been a lot longer than two hours."

Nick smiled to himself. "I got tied up. Besides, I thought if I gave it enough time, most of your company would get bored and leave. Are you alone?"

"Yeah, they all left. They'll be pissed if I don't get them back."

"Okay, go get your sergeant, but him only. I don't have time for a full quorum."

There was a short break. Mario came back on the line.

"Do you have the recorder going?" asked Nick.

"This is Sergeant Ruiz. Who are you?"

"Let's dispense with the grilling. I'm not giving you my name, and this is a burner phone. It'll be in the trash two seconds after I hang up. Let me fill you in.

"The two guys you got last night are part of a drug gang contracted to kill people. Officer Cava was on their list. They killed a couple of cops in Albuquerque last week. There were three members in that group. Now they're all dead, including the two from last night. There may be others involved." Nick was careful to leave out Kiki's family. Inquiry there would lead directly to her. It wasn't time for that yet.

"My partner and I are going after more hitters. The common thread behind these deaths is the victims have ties to the military stationed in the Middle East. I'm sure you've figured most of that out."

"Yeah, we had that this morning. Your partner was the one behind the rifle?" asked Ruiz.

"Yeah."

"How did you get onto this?"

"No grilling or I hang up. I know you're going to contact Homeland Security and the FBI if you haven't already. At some point, we'll have to deal with them. We both know that to get more information, they'll lock us up. I don't rule out waterboarding, so we're not anxious to talk to them."

"They wouldn't do that to U. S. citizens!" exclaimed Mario.

"Wanna go in there with me?" asked Nick. There was silence.

Mario squirmed at the thought. His brother had described some of the interrogations.

"Things would be a lot better if you worked with them," said Ruiz.

"Oh we will, eventually." Nick hung up. He pulled the battery and sim card out of the phone.

"That was interesting," said Kiki from overhead. "They put things together pretty fast. They may have already tied my family in with this string. The beheadings are the same MO."

Nick drove up the ramp onto I-10. "I'm not going to give them that yet. It gets too close to us. Let's call Juan."

Nick spoke Spanish like a native. "Juan, we'll be in El Paso in three hours. What are the arrangements?"

"Pick up the package at the Pemex station nearest the border. What are you driving?"

"We're in a van, but you have the connections and system for 'importing'. We don't. Let's meet on the U. S. side."

"Ay cabrón. Okay. You are correct. I'm used to Joaquin, he used to carry for us, so he knows what to do. Okay, the Walmart parking lot in three hours. Park on the far side. Flash your lights as you enter."

"I'm going to send my girlfriend for the exchange. I'll keep a watch for problems."

"Ay cabrón. Okay. There won't be problems from our side."

From the motorhome, Nick checked the parking lot through the night vision scope on the M1-A. The perimeter was deserted and dark. Nick watched Kiki drive in, flash her lights, and park. She sat for several minutes.

"See anything, Nick?" she said over the com system.

"Nothing yet."

Kiki primped her blond wig and pretended to put on makeup using the van's mirror. She was really looking at the lot behind. She hoped she looked like a bleached Mexican whore. That was the intent. Headlights froze her like a deer.

The black SUV pulled alongside. "You with Ricardo?" asked the heavyset Mexican in Spanish. His companion held a pistol across his chest.

"Si." She pushed the button to open the side door facing the SUV.

The passenger, a muscular man in black, got out and placed an athletic bag in the van. He glanced at Kiki, appraising her like a toy. He had on his tough guy look.

She smiled at him. "Gracias."

The SUV rolled away. Nick watched it exit the parking lot. "That went well." He kept the scope moving, checking out the exits and scoping the darkness. Caution when in the enemy's territory, a lesson learned in the Sandbox.

"So far so good. Follow me back onto I-25. Keep my six covered. Let's head to Truth or Consequences for the night."

# Chapter 7

Detective Mike Wong looked at Albuquerque Detective Johnny Cano across the conference room table. They were quite the contrast. Wong was of Asian heritage, Cano was of Mexican, tan with a black moustache.

Wong had left Tucson at six am for the seven-hour drive. With only a stop in Lordsburg for a bite to eat and bathroom break, his head was buzzing. He had called from the road. Cano was waiting for him when he arrived. Both wasted no time on idle chitchat. They had exchanged what information they had on the two crimes. It was time for the conference call with the Tucson Police office. The speakerphone sat on the table.

"Is your department treating this cop killing, this ambush as an isolated incident?" asked Lieutenant Hernandez.

Cano frowned. "We had no prior attacks, and the incidence rate across the country gives no indication of a pattern. So, yeah, we are. With the attempt in Tucson, that may change. We're looking into the background of the officers to be sure there weren't any ties or grudges. We have nothing so far.

"We're also looking into drugs. One of the officers was working with DEA for a while. So far, he's clean.

"The attack in Tucson has similarities – high caliber weapons, an ambush of a cop. It could be a pattern."

"Our attempt in Tucson might be considered isolated, except for the guy with the card," offered Hernandez. "We might have a series of attacks starting."

Cano frowned. "We got nothing from our scene, not even DNA. The only thing left behind was bullets. Where are you on the ballistics testing?"

Hernandez coughed. "We're working on it now. Get me your results, and I'll get you mine. A match may be the only way of tying our guys in with your scene. Any indication of more than two guys involved?"

"Nah. Our ballistics indicate two weapons, thirty caliber. The type commonly used in AK-47. We can't be sure if there was anybody else present."

Hernandez offered, "We had brass left behind. We believe the attempt was to fire from inside the van so the brass would leave the scene with the van. When the perp jumped out firing, brass went everywhere. Forensics says AK-47 style ammo," said Cano.

"We found two AKs with our perps, along with several pistols and a shotgun. Boxes of ammo were inside. We may be able to link that ammo with the bullets you have.

"Another incident of an attack at an isolated ranch occurred two months ago, but it doesn't involve cops. The mother and father had a daughter who was serving in the Middle East. Her husband and child were living with the parents. All the victims were beheaded.

"The daughter came back for the services. Katherine Russell met with the Sheriff's Department, but they were at a dead end. It frustrated her that the case was no longer hot. Nobody's heard from her in a while. The Sheriff's Department is treating this as case of smugglers taking over the ranch. It's uncommon, but not unheard of.

"There are similarities between your case and this one. The scene was as gruesome as yours, with the family slaughtered and beheaded. Different weapons, though. These guys used knives.

"A trace on the other weapons in the van goes back to the ranch owner. They were stolen from there." Mike Wong could hear the tension in his lieutenant's voice.

Hernandez continued. "I called a friend of mine with the FBI. They have better records of national incidents. Somebody's sending a message, but what and to whom?"

Cano grumbled, "With the FBI coming in, can Homeland Security be far behind? Good luck dealing with them. They'll push you out of the way and take over. That means they'll be moving in here, too. We'll gird our loins."

The image of dealing with federal agencies with huge budgets created a nervous ripple of laughter.

Cano looked at Wong. "What about this guy at the scene?"

Officer Mario Cava spoke up. "I never got a good look at him. It was dark, and I kept one hand on my Glock. When I saw the laser dot on my chest, it rattled me. I followed his instructions to set up the perimeter, then all hell broke loose. We were hunkered down behind that car with glass and bullets flying everywhere. Two loud bangs from the M-14 took out the bad guys. It got quiet, and when I looked for the mystery guy, all I found was the card."

Hernandez broke in. "We had a chopper there within minutes, but saw nothing. A few cars on the streets, that was all. He had to have a car waiting outside our perimeter."

"Any indication more people involved?" asked Cano. "What about the shooter?"

Mike was starting to like this guy. He asked the right questions.

"We checked the van and found another set of prints. So, yes, there was a third guy in the van, but not that night. Our county sheriff found evidence of three people at the ranch scene as well. Two sets of prints from the van match those from the ranch house. None of the prints came up, so we have no names or faces to go with them. These guys either were never arrested, or not citizens.

"We're looking into the shooter, trying to find records of anyone in the area with the skills to pull off those shots. So far, we've found no guys capable. The laser sight and accuracy lead me to believe he used night vision, military training."

"If they're after the bad guys, maybe we shouldn't look too hard," said Cano. He saw

Wong nod. A few chuckles came from the speakerphone.

"Detective Wong, do you see any reason to stay there?"

"I'll go over the crime scene reports tomorrow with Johnny and the CSI team, visit the scene, and talk to the neighbors. If nothing comes from that, I'll start back tomorrow. and I will stay in touch."

"Call me tomorrow before you leave," ordered Hernandez.

# Chapter 8

Nick held Kiki close as she shook in her sleep. Her eyes popped open. She stared at something only she could see. "Kiki, wake up. It's okay. You're safe here with me."

She turned her head and looked at Nick. Slowly, her eyes focused. She smiled and closed them, again drifting into sleep.

Nick watched her settle and her breathing deepen. Kiki's nightmares came less often, but were still worrisome. When she awakened, he'd ask her about them to see if she remembered, to see if they'd changed.

He'd fallen in love with her in Afghanistan. Her saving his life had a lot to do with it, but the times he visited her in the hospital were etched deeply. There was no blinding flash. He felt the love grow until now, he'd do anything for her. He was sure she loved him, maybe but not with the passion he held, yet.

Nick peeked out the window. It was bright outside, morning. And they needed to call Joaquin. He eased out of the bed.

The RV park in Truth or Consequences was sparsely populated because it was far from Elephant Butte Lake. That fit their needs well. Quiet with isolation. Tonight they'd drive to a rest stop near Belen, outside Albuquerque. Nick picked up Ricardo's phone and speed dialed Joaquin. He answered immediately.

"Where are you, pendajo? Why haven't you called, you asshole?"

Nick made noises, scraped the phone across the counter, and banged it on the table. He spoke unintelligible words, mumbling and slurring. He hung up. That would keep Joaquin guessing. The phone rang, but he didn't answer.

He climbed into bed beside Kiki and closed his eyes. He too needed rest, he too had dreams, but not nightmares. At least for him.

He drifted near sleep as the flashback formed. Nick was in the main hanger at basecamp when the call came in of casualties. An attack had overrun an observation post. It had been repelled, but they'd been hurt badly. He recognized the unit, a recon unit from their base. As he ran toward the medevac, the blades already spooling up. The zone was still hot. Two adjacent Apache attack choppers were also prepping to fly. The smell of fuel was thick.

Hot desert air sucked the moisture from his face. The trip over the barren landscape took forever. At last, the hill came into view. It lay outside a village of mud huts and dirt streets. The attack choppers zoomed ahead, guns blazing, rockets streaking into the area surrounding the hill. Figures scattered. Below the top lay several bodies. As the Apaches continued to circle, the medevac settled. Nick jumped out.

The closest soldier's helmet was blown away; little left of his head. He approached a couple of soldiers. One was sprawled on the ground, his head in the lap of the other, his eyes closed. Blood soaked his chest. The sand around him was crimson mud. The soldier cradling the other looked up at his approach. Nick was startled to see it was a woman. Her eyes were glazed. Her right hand held her Beretta pistol. Her left hand, rested against the fallen soldier's head. It was covered with blood from her own shoulder wound. The bubbling sound told Nick the prone soldier had a sucking chest wound.

The woman's lips were a tight line; she said nothing. Nick pulled the blood-soaked shirt aside on the prone soldier. The woman had placed a plastic bag over the hole in his chest as a first aid measure. But the continued bubbling told Nick the exit wound in his back was uncovered. Gently, he lifted the soldier from the woman's lap. Her eyes followed him.

Nick's partner joined him with a stretcher after getting the body of the dead soldier on the chopper. They lifted the wounded soldier onto it and carried him to the medevac. Letting his partner secure the stretcher, Nick returned to the woman. She watched him through blank eyes staring from a face smeared with blood, and powder residue. She was in shock.

At the rattle of machinegun fire and the whistle of bullets overhead, her eyes widened. She looked around, her Beretta sweeping the perimeter.

"We have to go. It's still hot here."

She looked past Nick, raised the pistol and fired twice. The muzzle blast caused Nick to jump sideways. His ears rang. The woman fired again. Nick turned to look behind him. A body in black pajamas lay still on the ground, His AK-47 in front of him. Behind him another black clad man struggled weakly to get out of a hole. Blood gushed from his neck. The woman fired again. He lay still.

She had saved his life. He turned to her. "We leave now!" He eased the pistol from her hand and helped her stand. She was only slightly taller than his shoulder. With his arm around her, he helped her to the chopper.

"Is anybody else here?" Nick yelled above the noise of the whirling blades.

She shook her head.

Nick signaled the pilot, and the noise increased. He felt the jolt as it left the ground.

In the air, Nick stripped off the woman's shirt. Her wound was a through-and-through. She flinched as he probed it. Shock was another problem. He laid her on the second stretcher, belted her in.

"Name, rank and serial number?" Nick asked, trying to bring her back.

"Russell, Sergeant, 505 13 2652," she answered automatically.

"Your first name?" he asked.

"Katherine. Call me Kiki."

"Kiki, this doesn't look too bad. How does it feel?"

"How's Dyke?"

"Who's Dyke?"

"Corporal Dyson. He's one of my spotters."

Nick glanced at his partner, working on the other soldier. Their eyes met. He shook his head.

"We're working on him. Who was the other soldier?"

"Corporal Ling. He took a head shot."

"Kiki, I'm going to give you something for the pain." Nick injected her and watched as her eyes closed. He pulled out his pen and marked an *M* on her forehead.

The hospital team was waiting when they landed. In seconds, they wheeled both soldiers toward the doors. Nick helped unload the body of Corporal Ling and began cleaning out the medevac. This was the hardest part. The rush of the evacuation and caring for the wounded was over. Now the immensity of the events settled in. Each of these rescues affected him. For those directly involved, he knew their lives would change.

After hosing out the interior, Nick walked back to the hanger, awaiting the next call. He wondered about the woman. There were rumors of a woman sniper named Katherine. She was the hottest sniper in the Middle East right now, with the most kills. ISIS had nicknamed her 'Iblis', a Muslim devil, and put a price on her head. The attackers had come close to collecting.

# Dead & Dead for Real

# Chapter 9

Joaquin screamed at his office wall. What the fuck was going on with Ricardo? His phone wasn't working, that was obvious. Where was he? With no word from Ricardo last night, he'd called Juan in Juarez. The package had been picked up by some puta. If Ricardo was fucking around, he'd have his cajones removed – slowly. The phone rang. He looked at the number. It was Ricardo!

"Where are you, you piece of shit?" he yelled.

The voice was barely intelligible, the words garbled, lots of noise in the background. "Broke down. - f ng van – rest stop - Walking Sands - I-25." The phone went dead.

"Fuck!" roared Joaquin. Their goddam car was broken down at a rest stop. He Googled Walking Sands. It was south of Belen, a drive of less than two hours. He had to get out there. If any cop came snooping around, it would be trouble. Grabbing his keys, he hurried past the bar.

"Marne, I'll be back in a few hours."

The beefy bouncer started to walk with him, but Joaquin waved him back.

The black Escalade flew down the interstate. Traffic was light. Everybody had stopped for dinner. As he passed the Walking Sands rest stop, he could see the parking lot was nearly empty – only one van and a motorhome. Why did that asshole Ricardo park next to the motorhome? Okay, maybe the motorhome parked next to him. He made an illegal U turn and exited the northbound lane.

Joaquin tapped on the van window. It whispered down, the business end of a .45 yawned at him. It looked huge. His hand dipped toward his waist.

"I wouldn't. Hands up." The muzzle bobbed up and down. Joaquin's hands rose. "Turn around." He complied. The door to the motorhome opened. A woman in the doorway looked down the sights of a Beretta pointed at him. Her face was a frozen mask, eyes flinty, jaw clinched. There was no doubt in Joaquin's mind she wanted to shoot him. "Get in the motorhome," instructed the voice behind him.

The woman backed up and motioned for him to follow. He heard the van door behind him open. He entered, and the woman motioned with the gun for him to sit at the table and stretch his arms across it. The man entered, closing the door. Sweat trickled down Joaquin's back as he leaned across the table. The man moved to face him while the woman covered his back.

"What do you want?" asked Joaquin. "I have money. I can give you money." He heard the pleading in his own voice.

"Keep your arms where they are so I can see them," said the man.

Joaquin felt the barrel of the woman's gun press into his neck. The man clamped his hands to the table, and Joaquin felt a sharp pain in his neck. "Wha…" Warmth spread through him. What the fuck did these people want? It was his last thought before blackness took over.


"That went smoothly," said Kiki as they stripped the inert form, piling his clothes on the seat, putting the contents of his pockets on the table for later. Together, they carried him back to the isolation chamber. Laying him in the warm water, Nick inserted the IV and attached the sensor pads. He checked the wall monitors and set up the drip. They closed the lid.

"You search his car while I hitch the van. I called in a reservation at the KOA in Belen."

Hitching only took a few minutes, and they moved the motorhome and van to the far end of the parking lot. Nick used a short ladder from the back of the motorhome to climb the parking lot light pole to the surveillance camera. He removed the tape covering the lens, and returned to the motorhome, staying out of view of the camera. In no time, they were back on the interstate heading north with their unconscious cargo.

# Chapter 10

"Lieutenant, I need to stay another day," said Detective Mike Wong. It was their three-thirty telecom. "We just got a call from the Staties. Buzzards led a rancher south of Lordsburg to a body. It looked like another hapless border crosser, but the fingerprints were a hit with those found in our van and at the ranch scene."

"Lordsburg! What the hell was someone involved with our attacks doing there? Cause of death?" asked Hernandez.

"He's on the autopsy table now. There were no signs of trauma, no wounds, nothing. He was pretty dried out, and the coyotes had chewed on him a bit. We were lucky to have a couple of fingers left to print. It looks like a heart attack, but we'll know more in a few hours. Tox screen and DNA samples are being run as we speak."

"We have this guy in our system," said Detective Cano. "His name is Ricardo de Silva. He's the brother of Joaquin de Silva, a drug gang leader here. They've been under a watch as a part of our drug interdiction program. With no arrests, we had no fingerprints on record, but his face is well known, even as chewed up as it was. It was his tats that clinched his ID." Cano opened a thick file. "Let me give you a bit of history on this gang."

"After the initial war over territory, this gang, Niños de Noche, established themselves in the northwest valley. They began to expand a few months ago. Our body count rose. Joaquin de Silva has ties to the Hijos de Hades drug cartel in Mexico. Hijos deals mostly in meth and pot. We're seeing heroin sales from them now."

"Did Hijos de Hades find another supplier?" asked Lieutenant Hernandez.

"Check with your fed contact. The heroin is not Mexican brown. It's white, so it's coming in from overseas. It may be a new player.

"Niños de Noche operates out of a strip club here. We know there's prostitution and drug activity going on and raided the club six months ago. No drugs and our undercover guys couldn't pin soliciting charges on them. We found underage girls working there, but the judge dismissed the charges against the club because the girls all had fake IDs, professionally done."

"Were they tipped?" asked Mike Wong.

"That's what we think. IAD is looking into it. Joaquin got popped for possession in El Paso a few years ago, so the club is in his brother's name. He'll have to find another front man now. We'd love to tie Joaquin into these murders and pop him."

"Did the CSI info we sent you on the other two guys help?" asked Hernandez.

"Again, no hit on the prints, but facial recognition matches two other gang members here less than twenty-five percent. The damage by the head shots was too great for better accuracy.

"So the question is what were Albuquerque drug gang members doing in Tucson attempting to assassinate a police officer and killing a ranching family?"

Once again, Detective Mike Wong admired Cano for asking the right question.

"We're asking ourselves the same thing," said Hernandez. "I'm meeting my FBI contact in a couple of hours. I'll let you know what they have to offer."

"Lieutenant, where are you on *Message Man* and the shooter?"

"We got a call from *Message Man*. He echoed much of what we suspected with regards to military ties of victims and intended victims. He said nothing about the ranch killings. Either he doesn't know about them or chose not to bring them up. The unanswered questions are:

One, how did they get onto these killers?

Two, how did they make the tie-in to military dependents.?"

An idea occurred to Mike Wong. "Lieutenant, have we looked into what the victims' relatives do in the military?"

Cano smiled at Mike. Good question, he mouthed.

"I can use my FBI contact to get that info," said Hernandez. I'm expecting a call from her any time.

"Detective Wong, let me know of any developments. I'll call back later. Thanks, Detective Cano." The phone went dead.

Mike looked at the file on the table and then at Johnny. "What do you think is going on?"

Cano frowned. "I think our gang is expanding their operation from just drugs to contract killings. That brings up several questions. Who are they contracted to? What's the connection with the victims?

"We don't have enough evidence to get Joaquin's phone records, but we can get

Ricardo's. The FBI can access Joaquin's. We might get an idea of what's going on."

"Let's visit the scene where Ricardo's body was found," suggested Mike.

"Four-hour drive. That'll put us there after dark, but yeah. If the Staties haven't made a mess of it, there might be something. We should get the autopsy results during the drive. We'll take my car. Highway patrol knows it."

# Chapter 11

Nick and Kiki sat in the chairs facing the isolation chamber.

"K, are you ready for this?"

She nodded. Was she really ready to hear of the mayhem wreaked on innocents by these monsters? The stirring of hatred arose, and she pushed it down. There was too much to do to let that take over. She glanced at Nick watching her. Kiki nodded again.

He keyed the laptop, easing back on the sedatives and increasing the stimulants to Joaquin, watching him wake up on the monitor. As he became conscious, his heart rate and breathing spiked when he realized he couldn't see, hear, or feel anything. His mind floated in blackness. He thought he was dead. Nick saw him strain to move, but the curarine had paralyzed him. He couldn't move. He yelled, but the sound suppression damped his cry so his ears heard nothing.

The monitor on the wall showed his heart racing, his breath in gasps.

*"Joaquin, you are with me."*

"Who is that? Who are you? Where am I?"

*"I am your God. You are with me."*

"Am I dead?"

*"You are no longer in your world."*

"What do you want?"

*"You must confess your sins to me, all your sins."*

"It's been many years since my last confession. I can't remember them."

*"Start with your last memories and together we'll recall your life. You must confess your sins if you are to be saved from eternal damnation."*

"It's not my fault! I was molested by a priest when I was an altar boy."

*"Do not lie to me. That is another sin."*

"Okay, I wasn't really, but he looked at me. It's been so long I don't know where to start."

*"Start your story just before you died and go backward."*

"I got a call from my brother. He was bringing me stuff and got in trouble, so I went to help him. When I got to where he tole me, two asesinos captured me and killed me. I didn't do nothing to them. Why did they kill me? They didn't ask me nothing or want anything. I didn't know them.

"They had Ricardo's phone, so they must have killed him too. Poor Ricardo. He wasn't the brightest estrella in the sky, but he was my brother. Will I see him? Did he get the chance to confess?"

*"What was Ricardo bringing to you?"*

"It was my payment. Powder."

*"Payment for what?"*

"Hijos de Hades told me to take orders from this cabrón to kill some people. They paid me with powder. La Sombra, he gives me expense money and the information on who he wants dead."

*"The orders came from this person?"*

"Si si. I didn't do nothing on my own. He did it. I just follow orders of La Sombra."

*"Who is this person who orders you to commit these sins?"*

"He's not Mexicano. That I know. He never give us his name. We call him La Sombra."

*"He would give you the names of those you killed?"*

"I didn't kill any of those. My men did it. I only follow orders. If I don't, I would be killed. This man give me a list with names, addresses, and information of the pobrecitos, poor people that he wanted dead."

*"You met him face to face?"*

"Si. He come to my house and give me the list."

*"Afterward?"*

"I call him to tell him it is done."

*"Did he give you a number to call?"*

"Si. It is in my pocket. He tole me not to leave the number on my phone, so I erase the call when we are done. He tole me to remember it and not write it down, but I couldn't."

*"The powder Ricardo was bringing was payment for this?"*

"Si. Hijos de Hades would get the powder and send me my share."

*"You don't think selling drugs to people is a sin?"*

"It don't say that in the Bible. It don't say that in the Diez Commandments. The people I sell to, they want it. I just do what they want. I'm giving them what they want, like Santa Claus. If I don't sell to them, they buy from somebody else."

*"But killing is a sin."*

"I don't kill nobody for a long time. I don't do that no more."

*"But you order it."*

"I don't do it."

*"If somebody refused your order to kill, what would you do?"*

"Why you talk about 'ifs? 'Ifs' aren't sins. Doing is sins."

*"Joaquin, search your heart. You know what is right and what is wrong. I will leave you alone to think about it. We will speak later."*

"Wait! Don't leave me."

Nick adjusted the drips. The monitors showed Joaquin's pulse and breathing slowing.

"That bastard accepts nothing as his fault! His confessions are hollow lies," Kiki exclaimed.

"It doesn't matter, K. Punishment isn't our aim. We want to rid the world of these bastards, and we need to glean every scrap of information we can from him. We'll let his God sort out Joaquin."

"Easy for you to say. It was my family he tortured and murdered," her voice harsh.

"K, we'll kill him. You can kill him."

Hatred rose within her like a black cloud, hot and stinging. "I want him to suffer!" A chuckle rose in her mind at the image of Joaquin writhing in agony.

"K, we're better than that. We're better than him."

Kiki pushed the hot hatred down. Nick was right. Her father and mother raised her better. She retrieved the slip of paper from Joaquin's pocket. It was a Phoenix area code.

Leaving the isolation chamber, they walked to the front of the RV.

"What else did he have?" asked Nick, as they sat at the table.

"A pretty good wad of cash, about two-thousand dollars. This looks like a safe deposit box key. It's marked ANB – Albuquerque National Bank maybe? Wanna check out what he has in there?"

Kiki held up Joaquin's driver's license and looked at Nick. "If we put a moustache on you and a hat, the bank won't notice the difference."

"Kiki, I'm six-foot tall. He wasn't even five-foot eight."

"Banks never look at height or weight – only the face. He might have some clues to La Sombra." Her voice rose as she smiled.

The sun was coming up. The night had been grueling.

# Chapter 12

Lieutenant Hernandez led the petite, slender woman through the bay of desks to the fishbowl conference room. Her tailored suit and no-nonsense stride was a contrast to the laid-back atmosphere of the office. She oozed confidence.

"Freddy, how are you?" asked Hernandez.

"Underpaid and overworked." A wry smile appeared. "The usual." She grabbed his arm. They stopped. "What's happening?"

"I want you to sit in on a status report on a couple of cases we're following. It appears to be interstate, maybe a possible RICO case. There may also be terrorist involvement."

"Wow, you have my attention. You said the three magic words."

They entered the conference room.

"Special Agent Freddy Foster, this is Officer Mario Cava, Corporal Klein and Sergeant Price." They shook hands. "The short version of why we're here is that two nights ago there was an assassination attempt on Officer Cava's life. It was thwarted by an unknown man who with a partner shot and killed the perps. He left this note.”

Hernandez handed her Nick’s card. She read it and looked up, awaiting more information.

“Other than the dead perps, we have nobody from the scene. The man and the shooter vanished. CSI found evidence in the perps’ vehicle tying it to a mass homicide near Red Rock where five people were murdered and beheaded.

“We have a detective in Albuquerque getting information on the cop killings there last week. The common thread between Albuquerque and Red Rock is the beheadings.”

“That is a pretty distinctive MO in the U. S,” said Freddy.

Hernandez continued. “What ties the assassination attempt of Officer Cava to the Albuquerque victims is that both have relatives in the military, serving in the Mid East.

“Let’s conference with my detective in Albuquerque and get the latest.” Hernandez called Mike Wong’s cell.

“Hello, Lieutenant.”

In the conference room, they could hear the sound of a car. Hernandez spoke. “Detective, Freddy Foster of the FBI is here. We need their resources on this. With crimes in Arizona and

New Mexico and drug gang involvement, this case may go federal. Where are you?"

"Detective Cano and I are driving from the site where Ricardo de Silva's body was found. The scene was too compromised for us to find anything useful. The Staties looked at it as an obvious accidental death. I can't blame them. From the photos, it looked like an illegal crosser got stranded. I'd probably assume the same. We looked for tire tracks, but everything was a muddle."

"Any word on the autopsy?" asked Hernandez.

"Yeah. Ricardo was on an IV for some reason. And it looks like an embolism killed him," said Detective Cano.

"An embolism? What would cause that?" asked Freddy, her voice rising.

"An air bubble injected into his bloodstream," stated Mike.

"Then this is a homicide?" asked Freddy, looking at Hernandez, who was nodding.

"Since there was no paraphernalia around, he didn't do it to himself. That's what the coroner ruled," said Cano.

"The lack of evidence is critical," said Mike. "The scene was staged. This place was remote, no witnesses."

"The coroner put the approximate time of death at forty-eight hours," said Cano, "but it was a guess. There were some strange things about the skin and the body. There were signs of salt residue and needle tracks, but they looked professional, not the usual drug abuser type. The tox screen will tell us a lot."

"He probably died after the incident in Tucson. That gives us a twenty-four to thirty-six hour window," said Mike. "It doesn't jibe well with the coroner."

Hernandez heard a phone ring in the car and Cano answer. After a few minutes, Cano came back on the line.

"Joaquin de Silva's car was found abandoned at a rest stop. No sign of him. It's on our way back, so we'll stop there. We'll call you when we arrive."

Hernandez heard the siren start before Mike hung up.

"Interesting case," said Freddy. "This could be a gang war, not related to the cop killings and attempted assassination of Officer Cava."

"Yeah, so the similar MOs of the cop killings and the ranch family are coincidence? When did you start believing in that?" asked Hernandez.

Freddy gave him a wry smile.

"Did you find other cases of military dependent deaths?" asked Hernandez.

"I did, but quietly. I'm not ready for the Department of Homeland Security to come tromping in here with their combat boots and tanks – arrogant bastards. We did have a couple of instances of military dependents attacked. Nothing above the normal stats of attacks. These two incidences change that. We're going to have to bring in DHS." Freddy shook her head.

# Chapter 13

The breakfast of steak and eggs was simple. Nick was cleaning up the dishes in the small kitchen of the RV. From the table, Kiki watched him move slowly. Their continued questioning of Joaquin had been long. The hours of tape would be of interest to the DEA and Albuquerque police, but Joaquin would not be available to testify. "What's our plan?" she asked.

"I think we both need sleep. That's my plan."

Kiki nodded. They'd been at it all night. She finished cleaning up while Nick went to check on their *guest*.

The IV drip would keep Joaquin out. By the time Nick returned to the front of the RV, Kiki was already in the overhead berth. When he climbed in, she pulled him close.

"I can't let them get away with this, Nick. I just can't."

"I know. Get some sleep." He held her until her breathing deepened, then closed his own eyes.

She moved within his embrace, trying to fall asleep, but her mind returned to Afghanistan.

She was back in the Sandbox. A low-flying helicopter rattled the hospital windows. Kiki was propped up in bed, IVs and monitor lines connecting her to the room. Her eyes fluttered open as Nick entered. She smiled at him. "Thanks for pulling my lame ass out of that mess yesterday."

"You're welcome. Before you ask, Dyson and Ling didn't make it. I thought you'd want to hear it without the bullshit."

Tears welled up in her eyes and spilled down her cheeks. Her jaw tightened.

"They're going to pay," she choked out.

"I know. Yes, they will. How's the shoulder?" he asked, wanting to change the subject.

"It fucking hurts!"

Concern crossed his face. "Aren't they giving you enough pain meds?"

"I want my mind clear. I don't want to forget what I've done."

"What you've done. What do you mean?"

"I was in command of that team. Their safety was my responsibility. I let them down, got them killed." Her fists tightened.

"The enemy had something to do with that."

"Yeah, but I chose the ground for the observation post," she snapped. "I didn't check closely enough. The enemy was inside my safe zone. I should have pulled back, but I was too anxious. I did it." Her chest tightened, her vision blurred.

"Kiki, it was a trap. The ragheads knew you'd be there."

"How could that be?"

"You were sent there because we received intel that troops in the town were massing for an attack. After we flew you out, the company went in. The base was abandoned. It was a setup. They were after you."

Kiki's mouth opened, but no words came out.

"Rumor has it that you're going to be pulled out now."

"Where will I be sent? What will I do?" Her voice rose.

"I don't know, but you're too hot to stay here. K, it's your ticket back to the U. S. You can go home."

She didn't smile. She felt as if the rug had been jerked out from under her.

At last, dreamless sleep came.

The ringing of Joaquin's phone awakened them. Climbing down, Kiki picked it up. "It's blocked," she said, handing the phone to Nick.

"Hola," he answered, placing the phone on the table in speaker mode. He and Kiki huddled over it to catch every word.

"You lied to me," said a raspy voice with a proper English accent.

Nick crumpled paper, creating noise. "My man, he lie to me." He faked a Spanish accent.

"What will you do about it? Your payment was made. You collected it."

Nick and Kiki looked at each other. "My man, Ricardo, he is taken care of. I will go to Tucson to personally attend to the problem. Then I go to El Paso to correct that."

"Forget El Paso for now. I have other names for you of more import. We must meet."

"You paid me for Tucson. I must take care of that. I will drive my mobile office. We meet at the RV campground at Picacho Peak near Tucson. I be there in three days."

"Call me when you arrive." The line went dead.

Nick looked at the number displayed on his phone. A phoenix prefix.

"Okay," said Kiki. "We have a plan. We'll have to work all night and tomorrow to milk Joaquin dry before he really does go to meet his God. Let's go to the bank first."

Nick looked at her. She was so casual about killing, yet she was so passionate and caring about him. The wrong side of her was not the place to be.

# Chapter 14

Hashim listened to the morning weather report from his bathroom as he got ready for the day. Hot, it was hot in Phoenix, like home. He looked in the mirror. He was fastidious in his appearance, his goatee carefully trimmed, black hair recently barbered. He had to maintain the air of an English businessman, and his neatness kept him on a level above those with whom he was forced to deal.

Speaking of which, his danger signal was going off. Joaquin sounded different. It could be the phone, the connection wasn't the best, but his accent was different, not much but... must be cautious.

Email this morning contained the names of twenty more targets on military bases in New Mexico, Arizona, Utah, and Nevada. Joaquin's gang was used for Arizona and New Mexico, and sometimes West Texas. Hashim must go to Las Vegas and Salt Lake City before the end of the week. Being relieved of the drive to Albuquerque was welcome. The outlaw motorcycle gangs had proven useful and reliable in carrying out attacks. Their infrastructure facilitated expansion. His friend Mohammed was coming to help in that expansion.

Since the murder of the family of the Iblis, Katherine Russell, the campaign of terror against the families of the infidels was beginning to reap benefits. Morale of the enemy was falling. The sniper was no longer in play, resigning from the military and returning to the U. S. after the death of her family. Another captain was reassigned when his cop brother in Albuquerque was killed.

Hashim toweled off the water and went to his closet. What to wear?

These targets were so soft, and the bikers and drug gangs would do whatever was asked of them for the pure heroin given in trade. Hashim smiled. This was an attack on American soil, and the effects would be far-reaching. Not as flashy as bombing attacks, it was a two-pronged program, with different goals. First was to demoralize troops and elicit a response. When the assassination program was expanded, the public would realize they were under attack at home.

The traffic in Chihuahua was slow. Mohammed needed a bathroom. The SUV pulled into a driveway with steel gates. He watched the gate open into a walled compound. Armed guards eyed him as he climbed from the black Ford Explorer, stiff from the drive.

The week-long ocean voyage aboard the luxury yacht was his only taste of extravagance. Yesterday, the ponga had met them off the eastern coast of Baja, California in a remote area of the Sea of Cortez. The wind was high, the sea rough. For two hours, Mohammed heaved the rich food he had eaten over the side as they sped east. His mid-morning arrival as a tourist fisherman at Puerto Peñasco went unnoticed. The rough seas shortened many tourist fishing trips due to seasickness. He joined other green fishermen on the dock, happy to be on land again.

The two men meeting him laughed at his distress. His dark skin, black hair and beard gave him a Latino appearance, and his companions kept speaking Spanish to him. The men loaded his large ice chests into the back of the car. The three men climbed in, and they left immediately. He was weary. With his rudimentary Spanish skills, he informed them he wanted to sleep.

From Puerto Peñasco, they drove south and east to Hermosillo, then east to Chihuahua. Mohammed could have traveled directly to Phoenix, but this roundabout route was to disguise his arrival, and get the drugs he carried into the hands of Hijos de Hades. It was important to maintain the chain of command with the cartels.

Kedar greeted Mohammed with a hug. Kedar stayed with Hijos de Hades, dealing directly with them.

"We eat fresh shrimp tonight," Kedar laughed, as they watched two men unload the ice chests.

Unknown to Hijos de Hades, frozen inside the shrimp packages was ten kilos of heroin. They believed their supply came solely from the Caribbean.

"Mohammed, you will rest tonight before your journey to meet Hashim. He is looking forward to your arrival. Let us go inside. I will show you the route you are to follow from here."

Kedar's room was neat but small. At the table, he unfolded a map. "Hijos de Hades will take you to Naco." His finger traced a path from Chihuahua north toward Juarez then east along the border past Agua Prieta. "A car is there for you. You will enter the U. S. through Naco, a small port of entry and easy crossing point." He smiled at Mohammed. "With your U. S. passport and story of working at the Cananea mining operation for an American contractor, you will have no problems. You must be clean shaven to match your passport photo.

"From Naco, you will pass through Bisbee and continue north to Benson and Interstate 10. This highway will take you to Phoenix. Once there, call Hashim. He will give you instructions to meet him."

"What about roadblocks, inspection stations?" Mohammed asked, worry in his voice.

"In Mexico, Hijos de Hades takes care of that. It is why we pay them. In America, after the border, there will be a stop. Just say that you are a U. S. citizen. You have a passport if they ask, and your English is perfect."

"How is the war in America going?" asked Mohammed.

"I so seldom get to talk to a brother." Kedar shrugged. "This is not the massive attack of 9/11 when we killed thousands in a single stroke." He held up a finger. "But it is directed against those fighting our brothers. America can never win against us."

Mohammed nodded. "They think there are rules of war. Rules favor the powerful. There are no rules for us. Hatred and fear are our weapons. We behead a few infidels, and their reaction is so predictable. People are tools we use to control governments. We strike at their civilization, not just them."

Kedar nodded. "For too long, foreigners have brought war to our country. This time we bring brutal uncivilized war to the land of the infidel. The American people will not stand for more decades of war overseas while killing rages within their country."

The two men hugged each other. They would be remembered for this attack.

"Whatever happens, Kedar, our homeland must be for us. Western democracy doesn't work in the Middle East. Arab Spring proved that. We will make the land too expensive in both dollars and lives for them to stay."

# Chapter 15

Speaking into the conference phone, Lieutenant Hernandez asked, "What did you find at de Silva's car?" He looked at the faces of the team he had assembled. So far, the investigation was a frustrating collection of dead ends. The police were one step behind at every turn.

Mike Wong and Johnny Cano huddled in Johnny's car. "It was cleaned out," Cano said. "There is no sign of him. No evidence of foul play, either. The only prints are his." Dust kicked up by the wind outside obscured the nearby interstate. Sand hissed against the windows.

"The forensics team left an hour ago," said Mike. "The weather's gotten bad. Dust storms are blowing the evidence away. We checked the tape from the security camera, but it was blocked, there's a gap. Whoever set this up planned it out. We're running the plates of the vehicles in the parking lot before and after that gap."

"It's looking like somebody grabbed Ricardo, sweated him, and went after brother Joaquin," said Johnny. "Couldn't happen to a better pair of guys."

"We're trying to get a trace on Joaquin's phone. Whoever has it pulled the batteries, so it's not showing up," Johnny Cano sighed. This was frustrating. "We got a short signal from Ricardo's phone yesterday afternoon near the town of Belen, but nothing after that. Records show he called from Truth or Consequences yesterday morning. We'll have a warrant for Joaquin's phone this afternoon."

"Could this be a rival gang?" asked Hernandez.

"Certainly it could, but then the attempt on Cava would be coincidence. I need proof of 'coincidence,'" said Cano. "It also doesn't explain any connection to our two cops killed here two weeks ago. The thing tying those incidents together is the note from your *'Message Man'* on the sidewalk and the shooter."

"Have you found out anything else about the ranchers killed a couple of months ago?" inquired Mike.

Cano smiled. Mike was learning to ask the right questions.

Hernandez answered. "We've been trying to locate the daughter, Katherine Russell, but she's disappeared. Nobody's seen her since the memorial service."

Corporal Klein spoke up. "We've got some background on her. She's some kind of hero to our troops in the Middle East. Known as Kiki or K, she was a sniper with the highest number of kills. The ragheads put a price on her head.

"She was wounded when her position was overrun. It was rumored to be an ambush set up in an attempt to eliminate her. After the ambush, command decided to pull her off the front lines. While in the hospital, she heard about her family. Being short on time before reup, she resigned and returned to the States." Klein paged through her file.

"The Pinal County Sheriff's office said she went over reports and the investigation with them. They were at a dead end. She's disappeared."

"You think it's possible she was behind that M1-A in Tucson?" asked Cano. He was already liking her as the shooter.

"That thought crossed our minds," said Hernandez. "We'll look for her a little harder, I think. Mike, any reason for you to stay there?"

"Sir, I can stay in contact with Johnny from Tucson. As soon as he gets anything on Joaquin's phone, he'll let me know." Cano nodded at Mike. "I'll start back in the morning."

"See you tomorrow." They closed the connection.

"Mike, this idea that Katherine Russell is involved feels right to me," said Johnny. "She's on a revenge mission. One question is who's on this mission with her? who was the guy on the street?" A partner, relative? he wondered. They'd check into her more.

"I have a lot more questions than that," said Wong. "But they're going to have to be answered by Katherine Russell and her mystery guy, the *Message Man*. So in my mind, the biggest issue is how do we get them to cooperate with us?"

Johnny Cano frowned. "Not an easy answer for that. I've been an Albuquerque cop for fifteen years, and I don't trust the system to find justice. They would be arrested. They've broken a whole passel of laws. If I were them, I wouldn't come in either."

"I know, Johnny. Whether you think of them as heroes or villains, when the feds get involved, they will disappear."

"We both know they're not done. Joaquin was not the jéfe in charge. They took him to find who to go after next. The ties of these murders to the military tell me there's international involvement. That really is for the FBI and Homeland Security, assuming it was our two who took him." A lot of unanswered question here.

"The Mexican cartels use the brutality of beheadings to raise fear and emotion, but so do the ragheads." Johnny shook his head. "It seems like we're devolving. At least some are."

"I don't know about Albuquerque gangs, but in Tucson when they do something, it's loud and visible to send a message. That wasn't the case with Ricardo. In the next couple of days, if Joaquin's body turns up in the street with or without his head, it may be rivals who took him. If he just disappears, I'm putting my money on Katherine the shooter and *Message Man*. We'll have to see who disappears next to find out more."

"Mike, do you believe in coincidence?"

Mike Wong shook his head.

"Me neither. I'm hoping Joaquin's phone records tell us something. Whoever took him has his phone. Joaquin might have heard from the man behind the assassinations. He'll be the next one on the hit list, if they've been able to get the information from Joaquin. If we find out who and where this next victim is, I wouldn't object if we were a little late getting to him. It would save the taxpayers a lot of money."

Cano laughed. "Yeah, what a shame if we were too late to catch our shooters, too."

# Chapter 16

Nick looked at the Walking Sands Rest Stop closely as they passed it on the interstate. He turned to Kiki. She was focused on guiding the RV through the winds that rocked and pushed it.

"Joaquin's car is gone. The cops are moving fast," observed Nick.

Joaquin's safe deposit box had proven a treasure trove. Inside was two-hundred-thousand dollars in cash, diamonds, and a kilo of heroin. It was obviously his bolt bag in case he had to flee.

Nick picked up Joaquin's phone and speed dialed La Sombra, their next contact. There was no answer, so he left a message trying to imitate Joaquin's voice.

"Just to be cautious, I ditch this phone. Here's my new number." He read the number from the burner phone they'd picked up that morning. "Call me on the new number." Nick removed the battery and sim card from Joaquin's phone and tossed them out the window. He wiped fingerprints off the phone. It followed a mile later.

"You could have called him on the burner. The cops will see this call when they get the records."

"I know," said Nick, "but he wouldn't recognize the number – might not answer."

Kiki nodded approval. "Let's take the back road and get off the interstate. We gotta get rid of Joaquin anyway, and there's more empty land west of Socorro."

"Yeah," agreed Nick. "We have plenty of time."


The climb up the pass was slow. A breakdown of the motorhome would be bad. After passing Quemado, they took a detour north, stopping at a roadside monument. They were alone.

"K, you want to kill him?"

He held his breath. Her touch of evil with Ricardo had scared him. For a few seconds, her eyes narrowed, her jaw tightened, her expression became intense. Nick stiffened as he watched emotions play across her face. With her lips a thin line, she shook her head. He knew he had never felt the intense hatred she displayed. He never wanted to wear her shoes.

He injected the fatal air bubble into Joaquin. When the monitors were flat, they removed him from the isolation chamber and dressed him in second-hand clothes from Goodwill. They deposited him in a culvert under the dirt road. With any luck, coyotes or wolves would gnaw on him and obscure his identity, at least for a few days.

"He sure had an easier death than his victims," noted Kiki. "He didn't deserve that."

The burner phone rang. Nick looked at the unfamiliar number. He answered.

"Si."

"Why did you change phones?"

"I think maybe there's no reason not to and many reasons to do it."

"Good thinking, Joaquin. As you can see, I did the same. Where are you?"

"On the road. I will be on time. I call you when I am there."

The line went dead.

"Let's overnight in Pinetop," said Kiki. "The Hondah Casino has a good park and cheap food. It's pretty country, and we have a day to burn. I could use the rest."

"Me too," agreed Nick.

Kiki called to make a reservation. They were full, but she was number one on the waiting list. She looked out the window as juniper trees began to appear, the motorhome climbing the mountains.

"My family used to have a place in Pinetop. Dad would bring up our horses. Mom and I would spend the summer riding the trails. It was great to get out of the heat. Dad would come up when he could. They sold it a couple of years after I enlisted. Without me, I think the shine was gone. Chet used to bring Lindy up, but his heart was on the ranch." After the mention of her husband and daughter, Kiki grew silent.

The motorhome labored up the twisting road into the pines. Kiki watched the mountains rise around them and thought of Chet, her husband, and Lindy, her daughter. She loved them and missed them, but she wasn't cut out for ranch life and motherhood. Chet realized that and offered to keep the home front open in hopes she'd change and come back. Now it would never happen.

Nick's turn into the RV park broke her reverie. It was crowded, but a cancellation had opened up a spot. He checked in while she unhitched the van. She wanted to eat at Charlie

Clark's, one of the oldest places in town. By the time Nick returned, she was ready to go.

Being a weeknight, the restaurant wasn't crowded, and she liked their ribs. Nick ordered ribs too. Looking around, it was familiar; the décor hadn't changed at all.

With the sun down, the temperature had dropped, giving them a chill as they hurried to the van. The night sky was brilliant with stars, the Milky Way a swash of light. She would enjoy tonight. Tomorrow awaited.

# Chapter 17

Mohammed should be arriving in Phoenix soon, mused Hashim. Sitting in his home office, he logged onto his email. In the 'Drafts' box were the latest unsent emails from his bosses. Both they and he used the same address. By not sending emails, it afforded them a touch more security. At least that's what their computer nerd said. Hashim had posted reports keeping them up-to-date.

His leaders were pleased with the killing of K's family. The Iblis had dropped from the fight since. Killing her would have made a stronger statement, but getting her out of the battle had saved many faithful lives and raised morale.

He had hoped to report Captain Sabino's brother was dead. That would have to wait for Joaquin's call. The woman and two children in El Paso would also have to wait for Joaquin's call.

Hashim looked at the new list. One hit in Nevada and another in Utah. He would have to contact Andros, head of Charon's Children. They would carry those out. He and Mohammed would go to Salt Lake City later in the week.

He looked around the house. Yesterday he'd cleaned it to prepare for Mohammed's arrival. The house, in an upscale neighborhood, had three bedrooms, one was his office. There was room for Mohammed to stay while Hashim filled him in.

He showered, grooming himself as was his habit. He looked like a successful businessman – black hair, neatly trimmed goatee. From his closet, he chose a turquoise golf shirt and grey slacks. People in Phoenix were casual in their dress.

Hashim called Mohammed's phone.

"Hello," came the tentative voice.

"Mohammed, it is me, Hashim."

"I've been trying to call you, but got no answer. I am in Phoenix."

"I changed phones. The old one is gone. Where are you?"

"I am at the airport. I didn't know where else to go."

"Stay there. I will come and lead you back."

The two plotters sat at Hashim's living room table. "Pakheyr, Mohammed. Welcome to Phoenix and the land of the Great Satan."

"Manana tashakor, Hashim. Thank you."

"We must speak English, though I long for the music of the Pashto language. Any slip, and we could fail."

Mohammed nodded. The television was showing a soccer match, the volume loud enough to muddle their conversation, if anyone was listening. Hashim was sure no one was, but caution was a part of his life. Mohammed glanced at the game every few minutes. He liked soccer. A map of the United States was on the table.

Mohammed was clean-shaven, his black hair freshly barbered. He fit in easily, attracting no attention. Tomorrow he would set his computer up and a bank account under the alias matching his passport. The house was rented under an alias, so Mohammed could assume the lease when Hashim left.

"I will introduce you to Joaquin de Silva, leader of the Niños de Noche, the Albuquerque branch of Hijos de Hades. They carry out our orders in Arizona and New Mexico." Hashim indicated those states on the map. Mohammed observed intently.

"You were with Hijos de Hades in Mexico. In a few days we will go to Salt Lake City." He pointed to it on the map. "I will introduce you to Andros Gallen, the leader of Charon's Children.

They carry out our orders in Utah and Nevada." Hashim pointed to those states.

"As soon as you are able to handle this operation in the Southwest, I will start a new attack in the eastern U.S. Washington D. C. has many military bases." Hashim pointed to that city on the map. "The targets are so soft. Strikes near the halls of power will terrorize the *kaafirs*, drive them into action against an enemy they cannot find. Their frustration will be a joy to Allah. Morale will collapse when they understand that their government has not the ability protect them.

"After that operation is going, we will bring in another controller to take over. I will move to the West Coast and California." Hashim's hand covered California on the map.

"This crisscross expansion will complicate efforts for our enemies. When the public awakes, it will appear to be a nationwide attack." He clasped Mohammed's hand in both of his. "This is moving very well." He smiled to himself, very well indeed.

"Tomorrow we will meet Joaquin. Hijos de Hades in Mexico are his supplier of drugs and his leaders. His instructions come from us, but the drugs must flow through Hijos de Hades. It is important to keep Mexico in the line."

Mohammed watched intently. He must absorb everything. His hands moved over the map. "The land is so big."

"Yes, and it is rich. The people are decadent and soft. They care only for things and money. The infidels have no God and no morals. And they are trying to make us over in their image and steal our land."

Hashim smiled at Mohammed. It would be good to have a partner, even if only for a while. It would be good to have somebody covering his back.

# Chapter 18

Nick cuddled up to Kiki. Her breathing became regular, he felt her relax. His eyes closed. He was so tired. They had been up for twenty-four hours. He willed himself to relax. Tomorrow there would be time enough to worry. But sleep eluded him as his recurring memory surfaced.

It was the day he told his family he'd be leaving. Nick watched the shock on his father's face.

"You joined the Army? Nick, why would you do that before you finished pre-med?"

"Dad, I wanted to do something on my own. When I get out, I can go back to school on the GI Bill."

"We'd pay for school," his dad stormed.

"Of course we would," echoed his mother, tears appearing in her eyes.

He knew this would be the reaction, but it didn't soften the blow of seeing his parents upset.

"Mom, Dad, I've been sheltered. You've set the path of my life: go to pre-med, enter med school, join Dad's practice, take over when he retires. I have to break out, go my own way."

"I thought that's what you wanted," said his dad.

"I don't know what I want. This will give me a chance to find out."

"But the Army!" his mother said, her words dripping with sarcasm. "You can do so much better than that." Her mouth opened. "You could get killed," she whispered as she realized that.

Doctor Sabino looked around his study, diplomas on the wall, medical books on the shelves. He seemed lost for a few minutes. "I can pull some strings, keep you out of the Middle East."

"No, Dad. On my own. I have to do this on my own."

Flashes of boot camp played through his mind, then the day medic was announced as his MOS. Medic! He would be sent to school to become a medic. It seemed appropriate. All his life he'd watched his father help people. That desire was in his blood. He found the school easy. At graduation, he was assigned to a medevac chopper, his unit going to Afghanistan.

His last visit home was tearful, fear in his mother's eyes, concern on his dad's face. He <u>would</u> come back.

He was at the field hospital, his first assignment in country. Keeping him in base camp gave him a chance to acclimate. The weather was like Arizona, but hotter. His view changed. As the new guy, he was hosing out a Humvee hit by an RPG. Blood coated the interior, the red stream of water running onto the already stained concrete.

The medevac raced over the desert, the hot wind burning his face as it blew through the open door. His first trip outside. A column of vehicles hit by IEDs appeared below, two troop carriers ripped apart ... three trips hauling out the wounded, the ping of ground-fire striking the helicopter on the last trip.

Later, sitting in the mess hall staring at his food untouched, his hands were too shaky to eat.

The mind adapts. After a month, the shakes had gone. He did his job. He now flew with his second chopper pilot, the first wounded by small-arms fire. The days blended together, he no longer counted them. Suddenly, his tour ended, he returned to the States.

Home was different after what he'd seen and done. Doctor Sabino understood, his mother never could. He knocked around Casa Grande until the boredom became too much, then he volunteered to go back for a second tour.

It was different. He knew what to expect, knew what to do. There was a new element though. They were on the offensive, retaking towns captured by ISIS, treating not only soldiers but civilians. He found the work gratifying.

And then he met Kiki.

The call for medevac spurred him to action, sprinting for the chopper, ducking under the blades, supply bag in hand. The blur of desert beneath the helicopter, the reassurance of the two Apache attack choppers on each side, the hot wind searing his face.

The helicopter banked and circled a small hill. A small recon group had been attacked. The three people were visible. The medevac landed while the Apaches circled, keeping the attackers at bay. One soldier was obviously dead, a shot through the helmet.

The two others huddled together. One was on the ground, blood soaking through his cammies, a chest wound. Nick checked him. Not good. He motioned for the other medic to bring a stretcher.

The other soldier cradled his head with one good arm, the other drenched in blood, a shoulder wound. He looked at the bloody shoulder, then into the soldier's face. He was stunned – a woman!

Only after he had her safely in the hospital did he learn she was 'K, The Sniper', nicknamed 'Iblis' the devil, by her enemies. The rumor was that the 'K' stood for killer because she had the second highest kill numbers in the Army. He knew the 'K' was short for Kiki, which was short for Katherine.

During his second visit to the hospital, he learned they both were from Arizona, her ranch only fifty miles from Casa Grande. They were neighbors. He visited daily. Nick liked Kiki, but she made it clear nothing beyond friendship was possible. She was true to her husband.

They talked of life in Arizona. Casa Grande was an agricultural town, ranching and farming the main industries. Nick told her of growing up, life as a doctor's son.

Kiki told him of her life, ranching, hard work, outdoor life. She longed to leave it. Her heart wasn't in ranching. She wanted to go places. She and her husband, Chet, had known each other since high school. Their romance and marriage were inevitable.

Things on the ranch got tough, beef prices barely met costs, so she joined the National Guard to bring in extra money. During basic training, her talent as a sniper came out. Expert rifleman was only part of the job. She had the ability to blend into the landscape, hide for days at a time, and assess situations. She could stay frosty under heat. Kiki was a natural for Recon. She enlisted regular army.

Leaving her family for a tour of Afghanistan was hard but what she'd trained for, and she proved very good at it. This was her second tour.

Nick was helping her pack her meager belongings for her discharge from the hospital and return to duty when a knock on the door interrupted them. Major Adams entered, the company chaplain with him.

Kiki and Nick looked at each other. This wasn't good.

"Sergeant Russell, I have bad news. We just received word from the Pinal County Sheriff's Office that there's been a problem at your home in Arizona."

"A problem? What kind of problem?" she said, looking from the major to the chaplain.

"There's no easy way to say this. Somebody attacked your family. There were no survivors."

Kiki's mouth fell open. She froze. Nick watched her crumble. He caught her and sat her on the bed. She grabbed his hand tightly. The chaplain came over, but she waved him away.

The major spoke again. "Sergeant Russell, we're pulling you out of the Middle East, sending you home. You're short, only a month until reup. Take some leave. Figure out what you want. If you want out of the Army, you can ask for a discharge."

He turned to Nick. "Can you stay with her for a while?"

Nick nodded, looking at Kiki. The major and the chaplain left.

Kiki's eyes were vacant. She was mute. Nick took her in his arms as her body started shaking. He held her.

The day had faded as they sat together. She looked up at him.

The depth of misery he saw tore at him. "I'll help you, K."

"Nick, I've lost my family, They're taking me away from my unit. I don't have anyone to go back to. What now?"

He sat with her for hours until she fell asleep. Nick curled up on the floor next to the bed. He didn't want her to wake up alone.

The images faded into black as he slept at last.

# Chapter 19

Kiki and Nick woke up in each other's arms. They made love slowly, enjoying the cool temperature and quiet of the White Mountains. It seemed like the lull before the storm.

They left Hondah before sunrise. Kiki drove the RV the back way, through the Indian town of White River. This route held less traffic though it was a little longer. Neither of them spoke much. The Salt River Canyon was spectacular in the morning sun. At a viewpoint, they stopped and ate.

The town of Globe came and went as did Superior and Florence. Kiki turned onto the Park Link, taking them toward the mountainous spike of Picacho Peak. By noon, they were in a space at the RV park. The park was nearly empty, winter visitors fleeing for cooler climes.

Nick called La Sombra. "I am here, the RV park at Picacho Peak. How soon you arrive?"

"I will be there in ninety minutes. How do I find you?" asked the husky voice.

"When you enter the park, call me." The phone went dead.

"Kiki, let's unhitch the van and park it in the next spot. We'll set up the tent as if it's another campsite."

"What's your plan?"

"We're going to tase him when he knocks at the RV door. You get under the van, out of sight. It's an easy shot, not even ten feet. We'll drag him in and dope him. Easy peasy."

It sure sounded simple, but things never were that easy, thought Kiki.

True to his word, the phone rang an hour and a half later. Nick put it on speaker mode so Kiki could hear through her com system. She was already under the van, a couple of ice chests on the ground hiding her. The Taser was ready.

"I have arrived at the park. Where do I go?" asked Hashim.

"The green motor home in the back corner. Campers are next to me in a tent with a white van. Park in front of my motorhome." Nick watched the black Explorer ease through the park toward them. The window tint made it impossible to see inside.

Gravel crunched as the SUV stopped. From under the van, Kiki saw La Sombra's wingtip shoes as he walked toward the door. Then she saw a second pair of shoes, Nikes. Oh Shit! There were two of them! She only had one shot. He would know it was a setup as soon as Nick opened the door. Shit shit shit! She had to hit one of them. Nick might take out the other.

Kiki peered between the ice chests over the barrel of her Taser. The well-dressed olive-skinned man knocked at the door. La Sombra, she assumed. The second man was not large. He wore casual clothes and stood behind La Sombra like a bodyguard, blocking Kiki's shot. Nick opened the door, Kiki shot the second man. He dropped like a sack of flour. The first man turned at the sound. As if by magic, a small automatic was in his hand. He fired through the open motorhome door. Oh, God! Nick!

Kiki scooted to the opposite side of the van, getting out. Before she could pull out her own Beretta, a crashing blow knocked her unconscious.

Nick peeked around the cabinet through the door. The bullet had missed. The olive-skinned man held Kiki by the hair, using her slack body as a shield. Blood ran down her face from a gash in her forehead. He fired another shot at Nick, then ran to the Ford, threw her in. The engine roared and gravel sprayed as he sped out the gate. Nick stood over the second man watching the car disappear, his heart sinking, rage rising.

He dragged the paralyzed semiconscious man inside, trussed him with plastic handcuffs, and gagged him. The hypodermic meant for the first man would immobilize the second for hours. Nick closed and locked the motorhome door and raced for the van. He wouldn't lose his prey. There was only the interstate, and he would be going toward Phoenix.

Interstate 10 was well patrolled, so La Sombra wouldn't speed lest he get stopped. Nick could creep up on him.

They were in deep trouble. I need help, he told himself. We need help.

# Chapter 20

Hashim kept his speed slightly above the seventy-five mile per hour limit. It wouldn't do to get stopped by a cop. He cursed himself for not listening to the danger whispers he heard. They never failed him before. He walked into the trap with Mohammed. If he'd been alone, he would have been captured.

They had Mohammed, but who were they? Not the authorities who would use many more men. They would have surrounded and tried to capture them. He and Mohammed were not to be taken alive, yet they now have Mohammed, maybe alive. Hashim didn't know if they used a Taser or a silenced pistol.

He looked at the woman crumpled in the passenger seat. She moaned as he pushed her forehead to one side to get a look at her. Through the blood running from her head, the face looked familiar. He reached over and pushed her hair to one side. His eyes widened as recognition dawned. He knew this woman. This was K, the fabled sniper. The Iblis!

He owed her a great debt. Through her success against his brothers, this plan had been born. He, Hashim, was given the honor of carrying it out. It was his chance to prove himself worthy of Paradise. Her family had the honor of being the first to die in this campaign.

She was submissive like a woman. She fought like a man. If she were a man, he'd have great respect for this warrior. She sought revenge in the way of his people, thwarting part of his plan and hunting him.

Now Allah had given him the opportunity for revenge. She moaned again. He hit her with his pistol. She collapsed, unconscious. He would have to stop and secure her. There was no doubt the man would pursue him, but the motorhome would be easily spotted.

Who was the person, this man? Was he a friend, a lover, a brother? Not a husband, Joaquin took care of that. Were there more of them? Hashim glanced in the mirror. No motorhomes were following. He would take her back to his house, but he must leave Phoenix soon. They had Mohammed, but was he dead or alive? Hashim could not chance that Mohammed was dead.

He had a few hours to question the woman to find out who these enemies were. He would enjoy that.

It was now obvious that his network with Niños de Noche was gone. Once again, he had ignored the signs. He would go north to Utah where the biker gang, Charon's Children, worked for him. He could find another gang through Hijos de Hades for Arizona and New Mexico.

Ah! Mohammed knew too much of Hijos de Hades. How long could he hold back his information? In Afghanistan, the strong lasted a couple of weeks. Mohammed was very strong. He had been trained to resist interrogation. Yet, he would break. It was inevitable. Hashim had a day, maybe two to tie up loose ends and get out. He must notify Hijos of the danger. Mexico was different. Hijos could buy their way out of danger. They owned the authorities.

He scanned the road behind him again. No motorhome. At an isolated exit to local farm roads, he pulled off. Out of sight from the highway, he used plastic wire ties to secure the woman's hands and feet. With a gag, he threw her in the storage compartment under the seat. Back at the overpass, he again checked the road. No motorhome in sight. He merged with the flow of traffic.

# Chapter 21

"911, what is your emergency?" said the operator.

"I witnessed an abduction. Connect me with the Tucson Police Department," Nick said.

"One moment, please."

"Tucson Police Department. How may I direct your call?"

"Connect me to Officer Mario Cava."

"He's in a meeting."

"This is an emergency."

"I'll take a message."

"This is a matter of life or death. It involves a cop killing. It's critical I speak to him."

"One moment, please."

"Officer Cava speaking."

"Officer Cava, this is the man who saved your life two weeks ago. Do you remember?"

"Yes. I remember." Cava looked around the table at the task force members: Lieutenant Hernandez, Detective Wong, Corporeal Klein. In addition, FBI Special Agent Freddy Foster, and Homeland Security Agent, Jack Adamson, were now part of this effort. He waved his hands to get their attention.

"Cava, I need help."

"I'm in a meeting about that and other incidents. I'm going to put you on speakerphone."

"Who is this?" asked Agent Adamson.

"Officer Cava can tell you more about me later. For now, I am in pursuit of the terrorist responsible for the cop killing in Albuquerque, the family massacre in Marana, and the attempt on Officer Cava's life. This man has captured my partner and is on I-10 heading for Phoenix.

"We believe he has begun a program for Islamic extremists to murder the dependents of military service people serving in the Middle East."

"Who is 'we' and who are you?" bellowed Adamson .

"Agent Adamson, my partner and I saved Officer Cava's life. We tracked the perps' trail back to Albuquerque and understand that killing military dependents is the common thread linking these crimes. I'm chasing the man responsible. If he is not captured, he will go underground and continue his mission, terrorism in the U. S. I'll tell you who we are, but it's not important now. Either get onboard, or I'll hang up and do your job myself."

"You son of a bitch! If you …"

Freddy put a restraining hand on Adamson's arm. "How did you find this out?" she asked.

"We questioned one of the team sent to kill Officer Cava. He admitted the family massacre, the Albuquerque killings, and told us of the attempt on Cava. That's how we knew and stopped it."

"Where are you now?" asked Hernandez.

"I'm passing the Casa Grande exits. I don't think he's spotted me yet, but I'm going to have to drop back to keep from getting blown."

Freddy made a call on her phone. In quiet tones, she gave instructions.

"How did he get your partner?" asked Hernandez.

"We set a trap to capture him. He brought a partner. It was more than we could handle. He escaped. I have the partner."

"And he has yours," stated Freddy, looking at the faces around the table. "Is he wounded, unconscious, what kind of shape is he in?"

"It's a she, and she was unconscious when he fled. He's driving a new model black Ford

Explorer. I'm afraid to get close enough to give you a plate number."

Freddy signaled Hernandez. With hand motions, he told him to get information on Nick's vehicle.

"What's your vehicle description and plate number?" asked Hernandez. "We'll get assets to you and then find him."

Nick gave him the info. "Be careful. This guy is armed, and if threatened will kill her."

"Yeah, we got that. You are going to have to come in. You understand that. Who are you and why should we believe you?" asked Freddy in a pleasant voice.

"I understand. We always knew we'd have to work with government agencies sooner or later. This is bigger than we could handle anyway. It started out as revenge for the Marana murders. The Pinal County Sheriff was treating the case as a murder by smugglers, but the beheadings told us it was terrorists. Yeah, the actual killings were done by smugglers, but they were hired."

Adamson took a breath, ready to begin his tirade to take control again. Freddy shook her head and held up her hand signaling him to wait.

"How did you get onto these guys?" asked Detective Wong.

"My partner talked to the postman for the Marana ranch route. He remembered a strange car in the area and noted the plate number. It was a New Mexico plate. We went to the Albuquerque address. They killed the cops before we knew what was happening. We did manage to tail them back to Tucson. Captured one and took care of the others."

"Yeah, we saw how you did that. Nice shooting. We'd have liked to capture them and get more information," said Freddy. "So your partner is the daughter of the family killed?"

Nick hesitated. He didn't want to reveal that, but they'd find out anyway. He ignored the question. "The one we questioned was their boss. We got everything he knew. It's on tape."

"Was that Ricardo de Silva, the body found near Deming?" asked Wong.

"Yeah, you guys were pretty fast with that one."

"I suppose you have Joaquin de Silva too?" asked Hernandez.

"You were fast on that one, too. Uh, we had him, milked him dry. That's all taped."

"Where is he?" asked Hernandez.

"Do you really need to know that?" asked Nick.

"We don't want him to cause any other trouble," said Freddy.

"In spirit, he's joined his brother Ricardo. I'll tell you later where he is."

"You've been some busy bees," said Adamson. "I look forward to sitting down with you and your partner."

"Probably a lot more than we do," said Nick.

Freddy broke in. "We had a drone over I-10 watching a human smuggling group. It is re-tasked. We think we've found you. Change lanes and immediately change back."

He spoke on his phone again, nodded and spoke to the speaker phone.

"Yeah, we've got you. How far ahead is the suspect?"

"Black Ford Explorer six cars ahead of me."

Again, Freddy used his phone.

"Okay, we've got him. Drop back. We can take it from here."

"I'm not dropping out. Either you guide me and keep me in the pursuit, or I'll get back on his tail."

"Look, whatever your name is, let us do our job. Back the fuck off," said Adamson.

"I'm not leaving my partner," yelled Nick.

"Okay, we'll keep you with us, but stay out of the way," said Freddy. "We need to talk to you, find out what you've got, and make a team effort of this. Keep your phone on. We'll feed you directions."

"Okay," responded Nick. Yeah and you'll keep a trace on me while you're at it, thought Nick. He'd deal with that later. Right now, he had to do whatever it took for Kiki.

# Chapter 22

Hashim pulled into the garage, the door closing behind him. His danger sense was jangling again. This time he wouldn't ignore it. He donned jeans, boots, long sleeved shirt and leather jacket. His bolt kit contained a travel kit, passports with different IDs, spare clothes, cash, and a Browning Hi Power with three spare mags. Into the backpack, he threw his laptop, extra drives, two kilos of heroin, and a bag of cash. No time for the woman, he'd do her here.

He threw the tarp off the Harley on the back porch and strapped the backpack to it. Now to cover his tracks and kill the woman.

The pain in Kiki's head was monstrous. She pushed it into a ball and shoved it away from her body. The blanket she was under smelled of oil, grease, and sweat. Retrieving her boot knife, she sawed at the plastic cuffs. Cautiously she pushed on the hatch cover. It eased up. Through the slit she peeked out. The SUV was in a garage, nobody visible. She scrambled out. The noise of the garage door opening would certainly bring her kidnapper back. The only other door had to lead into the house. As the sound of footsteps approached, she climbed behind a box on a high shelf. The door to the house opened. She held her breath. The garage wasn't large. He would find her.

Hashim looked in the back of the Explorer. Shit, she was gone! He glanced around, looked under the car. There wasn't time to search for her. He had to get out now! The security panel on the wall looked like an alarm controller, but it was more. He entered a code and pushed the 'away' button. It beeped, the mechanical voice said, "Timer set. You have two minutes to leave the area." He didn't need to find the woman. The thermal charges would take care of her.

Hashim locked the garage door as he returned to the porch and the Harley. She was trapped.

The familiar *potato-potato* rumble of the Harley broke the silence as it started. He thumbed the remote, the back gate opened. Moving slowly to not attract attention, he eased down the alley. On the street, a police car passed him, moving toward his house. He'd made it.

Kiki heard the motorcycle leave. She peeked out, saw no one, and crawled down from the shelf. She tried the garage door – locked. She went to the house door – locked! He had locked her in. There had to be more. The alarm panel showed red numbers ticking down. He had booby trapped the place!

She had twenty seconds left. Looking in the Explorer, she saw the keys. Without hesitation, she jumped in, started the SUV and threw it into reverse. With screeching tires, it crashed through the garage door, careening across the street, slamming to a stop against a palm tree.

Kiki was stunned, her head resting on the steering wheel.

"Police! Keep your hands where I can see them." A rough hand grabbed her, dragging her from the car.

She was too dazed to move. Shadowy figures moved around. "Bomb," she mumbled.

"What?" yelled a voice.

"Bomb, house," she said.

"Pull back! Pull back! Bomb!" yelled the voice.

She felt herself being dragged behind the SUV.

Through her fogged mind, she heard a loud whump. She passed out.

From behind the barricade, Nick's eyes moved from Kiki to the house as flames erupted from the garage with a whoosh. Within seconds, the whole house was engulfed. Police pushed them back. She had barely escaped, he thought.

He watched as medics hurried toward her, lifted her onto a gurney. Handcuffs locked her hands to the rails, an oxygen mask was placed over her face. The EMTs wheeled her toward an ambulance and loaded her in. At least she was alive.

Nick had to get out of here. The police would be looking for him. Having his van description, he had to leave now. If he got picked up, both of them would disappear into the black hole of Homeland Security. He was Kiki's only hope of escaping. Their captive also awaited in the motorhome. With Nick locked up, he would die. Though Nick would probably kill him, the slow death of dehydration wasn't Nick's way.

Nick drove the van into a deserted medical plaza parking garage. He changed the license plate for a fake one. On the sides, he stuck large brightly colored magnetic signs saying, "Bustamonte's Burritos." A wide magnetic red stripe on the roof completed the disguise. It wasn't much, but the best he could do for now.

Nick got on the 101 loop. His phone rang.

"Hello," he answered.

"We need you to come in."

"Who's this?" asked Nick.

"This is Special Agent Adamson of Homeland Security. Don't make us stop and arrest you. We have your partner, so you might as well come in, too."

"Not yet. I have things to do first." Nick hung up. He took the battery and sim card out of the phone.

Instead of I-10, he took the freeway to Apache Junction. The police would be looking for him on the interstate, so he would head back via Apache Junction, and Florence. The Tom Mix Highway was lightly traveled.

After Apache Junction, there was little traffic into Florence, mostly pickup trucks pulling boats. It was growing dark when he pulled into a restaurant parking lot. Nick wanted a legitimate van license plate. With the ID cameras today, any passing cop car would know something was wrong. They'd stop him. He changed his fake plate for a real one from another van.

# Chapter 23

Once again, the team was in the 'fishbowl' conference room. Detective Johnny Cano of the Albuquerque Police Department was on the speakerphone.

Freddy opened the meeting. "Johnny, I know Detective Wong called you this afternoon to fill you in. We were close, but that doesn't count. To update you, we have a forensics team at the house now along with BATF. The house was well rigged. It burned to the ground. Whatever he used to booby trap it burned hot and intensely."

"No body, I gather," said Cano.

"We think our terrorist suspect escaped on a motorcycle. A local unit observed one leaving the scene. We haven't found the white van either, but that's only a matter of time."

"Any ID on the woman?" asked Adamson, putting his coffee on the conference room table.

Freddy brought up a file on her pad and sent it to those in the meeting. She began to read to them as they followed.

"The woman didn't have any ID on her, but her fingerprints hit. She's Katherine Russell.

Impressive background. Until a few months ago, she was a sniper in Afghanistan. Decorated hero, second highest number of kills. She's quite the soldier. It was her family that was murdered in Marana. After she received the news, she returned to the States.

"The Pinal Sheriff remembers her. She looked over the evidence, read the reports, talked to the detectives – disagreed with them that it was smugglers. With no new leads, their investigation is at a standstill.

"Russell asked for copies of the files. Being an open investigation, the sheriff refused. She was not happy and vowed to continue on her own."

Hernandez spoke up. "Sniper comes back from Afghanistan to the funeral services of her murdered and decapitated family. She disagrees with the direction of the sheriff's investigation, which is stalled. Two people with ties to the murders are shot from a distance. Another suspect is found dead in the desert. His boss disappears. It's obvious to me this is about revenge."

"Successfully, so far," said Cava, nodding.

"Though I tend to agree with you, Lieutenant," said Freddy, "we can't rule out a gang war."

Hernandez gave her a cold look. "Any idea who the *Message Man* is?"

"We're not sure." Freddy opened another file on her pad and distributed it. "Four months ago she was on a recon and support mission in Afghanistan. Her position was overrun. Her CO says the ragheads had set it up to ambush her. She had a reputation and a price on her head. Russell was hurting them badly. Her two spotters were killed. She was wounded.

"The medic who pulled her out, Specialist Nicholas Sabino, visited her in the hospital daily. The Army decided to pull her out because she was so hot. She returned to the States for the services of her family, didn't reup, resigning from the Army."

"So maybe they had something going in Afghanistan," said Adamson, a sly sneer on his face.

"According to her CO, she was pretty straight. He didn't think so," said Freddy.

"What about this Nicholas Sabino? What do you have on him?" asked Hernandez.

Freddy opened another file on her pad and sent it to those around the table. She read from hers.

"Sabino was short, too. He didn't reup and came back to the States. He's from Casa Grande, but his parents haven't seen him. They didn't know he'd left the service and returned to the U. S. It's a good bet he's in this with her."

"Any word on Sabino's whereabouts? Do we have him yet?" asked Adamson.

Freddy shook her head. "He's pulled the battery on his phone, so we lost the trace. There's an APB out. We're watching I-10 and other routes for his van, but nothing so far. We are not assuming he is returning to Tucson, so the watch is widespread. As of now, he's in the wind."

"We do have his partner, don't we?" asked Adamson.

"Russell's still in a private medical facility," said Freddy. "We have guards on her."

Hernandez interjected, "She and her partner killed people here in Tucson. We want them."

"They probably did that in New Mexico," said Cano through the speakerphone. "We want them too."

"She's property of Homeland Security," said Adamson. "As soon as she's discharged from the hospital, we'll take her into custody as part of a terrorist investigation. We're going to keep her and this Nicholas Sabino safe, when we get him."

He looked from face to face, assuring himself they had the message. Hernandez's mouth opened to object, but a sharp look from Freddy silenced him.

"I think Sabino will return to Tucson," said Cano.

Nobody around the table contradicted him. "Why would he do that?" asked Mike Wong. This should be good, he thought to himself.

Hernandez held up a finger. "They had a place where they questioned Ricardo. He was in Tucson." He held up another finger. "They were going to capture this terrorist somewhere south of Casa Grande." He held up a third finger. "They had to have a place to question him."

"What about Joaquin?" asked Mike Wong. "He was taken near Albuquerque. Ricardo's body was found near Deming. That argues that they are mobile."

"They do drive a van. Think they're working out of it?" asked Mario Cava.

Through the speaker phone, Cano said, "Possible. They could have taken Ricardo in the van on the trip to Albuquerque. It was lucky we found him. And there was enough left to identify him.

"They could have had Joaquin in the van, brought him back to Tucson for questioning. That would mean his body may turn up there. I also think they have a place near Tucson. It would be remote. They are extracting information. I don't know how you do that quietly from these guys. Noise would attract attention. Sabino will head back to Tucson."

Hernandez spoke. "We'll work with Pima and Pinal County Sheriff Departments looking in the Marana and Casa Grande areas for remote sites. That's a lot to cover. We'll keep an APB out statewide."

"One other thing," said Cano. "We checked with de Silva's bank. The day he disappeared, he accessed his safe deposit box. Bank videos weren't good, but they show somebody looking like him only taller. Whatever Joaquin had in that box, somebody else has it now. I bet a picture of Nick Sabino will look amazingly like the guy at the bank."

"Well," said Freddy, "we can assume that safe deposit box was his bolt stash. Probably cash, at the least."

"That's what we thought," said Cano. "Too bad. We were looking forward to that money. We will be going after his other assets."

"Of course you'll turn those over to the Bureau," said Freddy.

"Oh, for sure," said Cano. Only Mike Wong smiled.

# Chapter 24

As he anticipated, the Tom Mix Highway was deserted. Park Link was equally empty of traffic. Most of the few RVs at the park were dark when Nick returned.

Nick stretched a blue plastic tarp to make a shade and cover the van. He placed plastic chairs around so it would look like somebody's campsite. Tomorrow he'd have to do something about the van.

The captive had moved around the floor, struggling, to no avail. Nick sat him up. His yells were muffled by the gag. Nobody would hear him. Another injection rendered the small man unconscious. Nick undressed him and dragged him into the shower. He was a mess, having lost bodily control from the Taser.

Rinsed off in the shower, Nick hauled him to the back and hoisted him into the isolation chamber. The monitors and IVs were attached. Slowly the chamber filled with the body-temperature brine. Nick closed the lid and adjusted the drips to keep him under for the night.

He emptied the pockets of the captive's clothes, putting them in plastic bags destined for the dumpster. This guy wouldn't need them again. He had a driver's license and passport under the name of Michael Scott with a Phoenix address. It wasn't the house that burned. His wallet contained no credit cards, no pictures, and forty dollars. Around his neck he had worn a silver chain with a rial coin. It was the only jewelry on him. Whoever he was, he was not Michael Scott.

Nick had to keep busy, or he'd think about Kiki. Those thoughts made him sick and angry. He had to be sharp. That would come later. Scrambled eggs and sausage for dinner. As hungry as Nick was, the food was tasteless. He had to eat. Tomorrow his 'guest' would be questioned.

Nick had to come up with some way of communicating with Freddy and the cops without exposing himself. If they located him, they'd take him. They could prosecute him for the murders, but that wouldn't happen, because a trial would be public. It would reveal this terror campaign, and they didn't want that. The American public must believe their homeland was safe.

After eating, the exhaustion from the day hit him. In slow motion, he climbed into bed.

Sleep eluded him. The images of Kiki being dragged into the SUV, the explosion at the house, seeing her on the stretcher. It tore at his heart. He felt relief that she was alive, hopefully not seriously hurt. The concern was that she was again a captive – now of their own government.

Scenarios ran through his head, but none of them with happy endings for him and Kiki. She would inaccessible, under arrest but safe. At least he hoped so.

Could Nick go after La Sombra by himself? He and Kiki had failed together. They were going to have to work with the government. Perhaps he could bargain for Kiki's release. That was the only path with a chance.

At last, his eyes closed. He lapsed into a dreamless sleep.

Sunlight streaming through the window woke Nick. He reached for Kiki, then remembered she was gone. Yesterday flooded back, immobilizing him. Can't freeze up, he told himself. Busy day today.

He checked on his prisoner. The monitors showed a steady though slow pulse and respiration rate. Nick adjusted the drip slightly. He had to stay unconscious until Nick was ready to question him.

After stowing gear, cleaning out the van, and hitching it up, he headed the motorhome east toward the rising sun and Tucson. This early in the morning the traffic was light, so he arrived at the Instant Paint and Body shop before they were open. Parking the motorhome in a church lot a block away, he drove the van to a small café for breakfast.

At nine sharp, he walked into the waiting room of the paint shop.

"May I help you?" asked the young girl behind the counter.

"I want to get my van painted," said Nick, pointing outside.

"Sure," said the girl. She took him through the process of choosing the paint quality and color.

"Bronze," said Nick.

"It's one of our most popular colors. We can do it tomorrow."

"I need it now," said Nick. She held up her hand. "I'll pay extra." She held up a finger, her purple lacquered nail drawing Nick's eyes. She disappeared into the office.

The pudgy man who emerged looked Nick over. "We have a tight schedule. I can't do your car until tomorrow."

"I'll pay double, in cash," said Nick. "I'm going to a high school reunion in Nogales tonight, and I have to have it."

The manager rubbed his jaw. Nick put half the money and his keys in the man's hand. "I'll be back at three with the balance."

# Chapter 25

Nick parked the motorhome in a deserted part of the Costco parking lot. This early, there were many of those. With the curtains drawn he went back to the isolation chamber. The monitors showed slow heartbeat and respiration. He began to wake the man. Gradually, his vital signs increased. Brain activity and heart rate spiked. He was awake. Nick watched the monitor and listened.

The man screamed. Nick said nothing. The man's heart was racing. Brainwave activity shot up. He was panicking. Nick remained mute. A continuous wail came from the man.

"Where am I?" he yelled – his first coherent words – in Arabic.

Nick answered in Arabic.

*"You are with me."*

"Who are you?"

*"You know who I am. Do you know who you are?"*

"I am Mohammed. If you are Allah you would know that."

*"I didn't ask who you were."*

"Am I dead?"

*"You have left your world behind. You will not return. You have served me faithfully. To enter Paradise you must create a song of your life. It is how all will know you. Start with your latest memories and move back through your life to your earliest memories. Sing of your service to me."*

"I was with my friend, Hashim…"

It was painstakingly slow work. Nick decreased the stimulants, increased the sedatives as three-o'clock approached, Mohammed went to sleep.

The girl behind the counter with a smart phone stuck to her ear raised a purple fingernail as Nick entered the auto-paint shop. "Is my van done?" he asked.

"Gotta go" she said as she disconnected. "Yes, sir," She got the manager.

Nick handed him the balance of the money.

The manager handed him the keys. "Don't wash or wax it for at least three days," he admonished. "The paint you had wasn't in bad shape. Why'd you change it?"

"Bronze was my high school girlfriend's favorite color. It'll remind her of my old van and the good times we had." He winked. The manager laughed.

Nick drove his shiny van to a nearby electronic store.

"Shortwave radio? Yeah, we got some. You'll have to get a license before you go online." The clerk led him to the back of the store. "We got new ones, and a few used ones."

Nick looked through the inventory. His eyes settled on one. "How much for that one?"

"That's a pretty old one. You sure?"

"Yeah, how much?" Nick asked, digging in his pocket for the cash.

Heading east on I-10, Nick exited at the Karchner Caverns campground near Benson. There were only a few spaces left. He took the most remote. He set up camp, unfurled the awning, unfolded the picnic table, and set up the propane barbeque. With a beer in hand, he watched the chicken on the grill, nodding to neighbors who strolled by. It was pleasant, relaxing. He wished Kiki were with him.

After cleaning up, he went back to work. By midnight, Mohammed had sung his song. Nick knew everything Mohammed knew. Somewhere between here and Salt Lake City, he would meet his God for real. Nick wanted to believe it would not be as pleasant, but that was only hope and speculation. Before going to bed, he again exchanged his license plates for another sleeping camper.

Staring at the ceiling, he tried to plan for the next few days, catching up to La Sombra – Hashim. Nick now knew his name. Mohammed said they were to head north to another gang he was setting up to perform assassinations. There was a chapter of Charon's Children in Las Vegas, but Nick thought that was too close to Phoenix. He would go the main chapter in Salt Lake.

Before leaving Karchner Caverns, he set up the shortwave. As he approached Tucson he called Cava on Ricardo's phone.

"Officer Cava, do you know who this is?"

"Oh, yeah."

"In one hour, I'm going to call you on a shortwave set."

"What's that?"

"Go to your dispatchers, tell them to get it set up so all your federal buddies can conference in. I won't be using this phone again."

He gave him the frequency and hung up. He was hoping the shortwave would be harder to trace. It wouldn't do for him to get nabbed. That would spoil all his plans. Neither he nor Kiki would have a nice day for a long time.

# Chapter 26

The shortwave unit sat on the conference table, hissing at the empty airwaves. The channel they were tuned to was seldom used. Agents Foster and Adamson were not happy about the shortwave communication. It was so ancient that they had problems getting a receiver. Triangulating on the sender was even harder.

The voice startled Cava. "Are you there, Cava? Over."

"Yeah, we're all here. The FBI, Homeland Security, the TPD, and on the speaker phone, Albuquerque Police."

"Mr. uh… Nick, can I call you Nick?" asked Adamson.

There was a pause when nothing was said.

"You have say 'over' when you're finished speaking," said Nick, explaining etiquette. "You can call me whatever you want. It doesn't matter. Several things.

"First, I'm not coming in. Before she was taken, we captured a member of this assassination group. I've been questioning him, and there are some developments. When I'm done, I trade him and the tapes of my interrogation for her. Over."

"Nick, you're not in a position to bargain," snapped Adamson. "Come in and bring him with you. We'll work out a deal." He failed to release the talk button.

Lieutenant Hernandez's eyebrows rose. "Agent Adamson, these people committed murder. That's a state offense. You do not have the authority to bargain immunity for them."

Adamson turned toward him and held up both hands, signaling it was a ruse.

"Lieutenant Hernandez," said Nick, "we all know that Adamson's last statement is a complete lie. If I come in, I, whoever I bring in, and Kiki will all disappear. Your claim to me is way down the list.

"I have a publicity package on Katherine Russell extolling her heroic status that will be sent to the press if she is not released. There are a lot of soldiers in Afghanistan who would stand up for her. I will not let her disappear. I will also release the tapes of the interrogations. There are things on them that no administration would want public. So let's dispense with the lies, false promises, coercion, and trying to figure out who has the largest dick. There is some serious shit here.

"I have been questioning Mohammed el-Harabi. I'll give you an hour to access your records on him. In the meantime, Adamson and Foster, stop trying to find me. You won't. Over and out." Nick released the talk button. His hands shook for a few seconds. Why was authority difficult to talk to?

Nick started the motorhome, heading for Interstate 8 going west. His next call would be from Maricopa.

"I gather the gang's all there," said Nick. "What did you find on Mohammed? Over."

"Nick, you've captured a real bad guy. You have to bring him in. Over," said Freddy.

"Oh, he's no threat now. You'll get your chance at him," affirmed Nick. "But as you can see from his history, he withstood the worst Abu Ghraib threw at him. What makes you think you'll do better with the laws and oversight in this country? Over."

"He may not stay in this country. Will he be in any shape to talk?" asked Adamson.

Nick heard silence. Had he shocked them as they contemplated what had been done to get Mohammed to talk – and what would be done?

"Adamson, will you get with the program? Say 'over' when you're finished speaking and release the send button," admonished Nick. He enjoyed tweaking the puffed-up agent.

"He will be in perfect physical condition. I've done nothing to his body. His mind is something else. Mohammed was raised Muslim. Though not a strict devotee, his beliefs began as a child and are deeply rooted. Right now, he believes he is dead and conversing with Allah in preparation for entering Paradise. Imagine the shock when he finds out that is not the case. I cannot vouch for his mental state after that. None of my other inquisitions ended this way. Over."

Again, there was stunned silence as each person's image of facing their god after death arose. They already knew how his other sessions ended. Were there others he had done?

"What you are doing is illegal. Over," stated Freddy.

"That's funny coming from you. It's almost as legal as waterboarding," said Nick. "Let's not get into discussions of legality. We have other issues. Over," said Nick. He could picture the local law enforcement people squirming.

"What do have? Over." asked Adamson.

"From what I've discovered, Hashim al-Zaqiri is who we are after. I'll give you another hour to access records on him. Over and out."

Nick had to walk around outside, relieving the tension of the conversation before he could drive. The brilliant blue sky and the quiet of the rest stop calmed him. Time to get moving.

# Chapter 27

Hashim's back and butt were killing him. How did these bike riders take hour after hour on these motorcycles? His stop in Page, Arizona was as much to relieve his back as to escape the rainstorm bearing down on him. The hotel overlooked Lake Powell with the hoodoo rock formations rising from it. At another time, he would have enjoyed the view.

Hashim grabbed his gear from the bike and ran for the door of his room. The sun blanked out, and the storm struck with force. Lightning lit the sky; thunder assailed his ears and shook the walls. The parking lot disappeared behind sheets of rain.

Hashim toweled off and logged onto his laptop. He placed an email in his Drafts box. It was a coded message that Mohammed was dead or captured. Hashim did not believe it was government authorities, but some other agency responsible. He wrote of the closed-down Phoenix operation. He was on the road. His New Mexico contractors had been compromised. Hashim would send a full status report once established in his new headquarters.

Next, he checked the news.

*A fire at a Carefree home has claimed the life of at least one person. Officials continue to dig through the ashes seeking the cause. Preliminary reports blame arson. The identity of the body is unknown at this time. Witnesses reported the house was surrounded by police and SWAT teams preparing for a standoff situation when it exploded and was fully engulfed. Arriving firemen were unable to prevent total destruction. They did keep it from spreading to neighboring homes.*

Photos showed yellow crime scene tape surrounding the blackened brick walls, melted concrete, and little else. Rather than an explosion, Hashim had set thermite, which had burned hot, consuming everything.

He logged off, knowing the police would take at least a day of sifting through the ashes to determine he wasn't in the house. Normally, it would take more than a day to identify the body burned that badly as Katherine Russell's. With her

DNA in the military records, not this time. The search only required a match. Obviously, her partner had gone to the police, but how much did he tell them? How much would he cooperate? They were killers.

Katherine Russell was seeking revenge for her family, something Hashim knew well. He respected her for that even though she was a woman. Revenge was a tradition of his people. Would her partner seek revenge for her death instead of waiting for a court of law? How un-American.

Her partner was another concern. Hashim knew his shots at the motorhome had missed, or any wounds were minor. He had called in the authorities. How long would it take this man to find him?

Was Mohammed alive or dead? The silenced pistol shot had dropped him like a rock. If he were dead, then Hashim had time. If he were alive, how long would he hold up to questioning? Mohammed had been a prisoner at Abu Ghraib prison. He'd held out there. He was strong.

Hashim was tempted to pursue the partner, go offensive, rather than defensive. He would choose the grounds of the conflict. But his mission came first. He called Andros Galen, leader of Charon's Children in Salt Lake City.

"Andros, I will visit you in two days. We have business."

"Yeah, okay. I'll be at the club all day. Are you bringin' me anythin'?"

"I always do."

Charon's Children, an OMG, Outlaw Motorcycle Gang, was a chapter of Hijos de Hades, in Mexico. It was proving very useful. Like Niños de Noche, they were expanding into heroin from methamphetamines. These contract murders would be additional income.

Andros would be unhappy to learn of the demise of their Albuquerque brothers, though he might look upon it as an opportunity for Charon's Children. Gangs could be cutthroat.

Perhaps Hashim should let them take care of Katherine Russell's partner. Honor decreed Hashim should do it, but killing him by proxy was acceptable.

Tomorrow would be a long day on the bike. State Highway 89 would take him to Spanish Fork. From there it was an easy ride to Salt Lake City. He needed a house and a car. First, he had to establish his new identity, open a bank account, get business cards, everything to become a new person.

Worries about Mohammed nagged at him. Hashim had been lax in keeping up with his prayers, but he felt the need. He got out his prayer rug and went through the ritual. Afterward, he felt good, energized. He would do better from now on.

As he lay in bed, Hashim reviewed the last few days. First, Ricardo had failed to kill the Tucson cop. Of course, he had been successful with the Albuquerque cops and the sniper's family. Ricardo had disappeared. Then Joaquin disappeared, and now Mohammed. Katherine Russell and her partner were moving up the ladder of this mission very successfully. He was the next rung. The Iblis, Katherine Russell, was gone. Was she half of their force? He needed to take this threat much more seriously.

Mohammed knew of Charon's Children and Salt Lake City. This partner of the Iblis would come there seeking him. He needed to go on the offensive with assets in Salt Lake City. He would become the hunter – on his ground.

# Chapter 28

Nick left Interstate 17 at the Sedona exit. Fifteen miles down the road, he pulled into a scenic view parking lot. It was past time to contact the alphabet soup group again. FBI, DHS, TPD, and APD. There would probably be more added, Nick mused. At least he could look at some scenery while doing this distasteful job. The red cliffs were beautiful.

Walking around the motor home, as if inspecting it, he pondered what to reveal about Mohammed? The possibilities were troubling. The Middle East assassination program of military dependents for sure. Mohammed was the first real link. The drug connection was the payoff for the assassins. Kiki and Nick were after the assassins, not the drugs. Nick was sure the Department of Homeland Security would get nothing from Mohammed when he turned him over.

Mohammed believed to his very soul he was dead and going to Paradise. When faced with an alternative reality, one where he had not been with his God, that he was not going to Paradise, that he had betrayed everyone, revealing everything to his enemies, he would retreat into the reality of his death. Nick had seen into his mind. Mohammed would not respond to this ugly reality.

But Mohammed was powerful trade goods for getting Kiki back. Returning to the RV, Nick took a deep breath and turned on the shortwave. The empty airwaves hissed at him. He depressed the talk key.

"Are you guys there? Over."

"We're here. Before you go any further, this isn't secure. Anybody can listen in. Over," said Adamson.

"Who's there for this meeting?" asked Nick. "Over."

"I'm Special Agent Freddy Foster, FBI. With us is Special Agent Jack Adamson, Department of Homeland Security, Lieutenant Roberto Hernandez, Tucson Police Department, and we've brought in Dianne Coleman, CIA, because of the international aspects. On the speakerphone is Detective Johnny Cano of the Albuquerque Police Department."

"Hail hail, the gangs all here. I'm open to suggestions as to how we can talk without you trying to trace and capture me. I suppose we could use snail mail, but things are moving a little fast for that. Over."

"What if we gave you a secure frequency? Over," asked Freddy.

"That would be fine, but how would I get the equipment for that? You going to leave it for me at the Post Office? You think about it and let me know. In the meantime, let's talk about Hashim al-Zaqiri and what I want. Over." Nick sounded tough, but his stomach was heaving and sweat dripped from his brow.

"The CIA has much more information on him," responded Freddy. "Zaqiri is a despicable character and one we'd like to get our hands on. Can you help us with that? Over."

Here it was, thought Nick. Let the bargaining begin.

"I have information that may lead to him. I want him, too, so we'll have to reach an agreement. Key to that agreement is that Katherine Russell is released. We're a team, we work together. We will sign a contract that absolves us from any prosecution, past and while we are working for you. Over."

"You want a contract and free rein! Who do you think you are? I think we'll just keep your girlfriend and capture you. It's only a matter of time before that happens," sneered Adamson.

"Adamson, say 'over' when you're finished ranting. I thought you'd have that down by now. So while you're pursuing me, how many other military dependents get killed? That'll play nice in the press. Adamson, maybe this decision is above your pay grade. Freddy, should I be talking to somebody else? Over."

Freddy held up a hand to keep Adamson from blowing up. Lieutenant Hernandez was also shaking his head no. She understood the men trying to steamroll Nick, but the reality was that he held the access to al-Zaqiri. They might get lucky, but the downside would be more deaths and publicity none of them wanted. Freddy ignored them. She'd pass this up the chain of command. Let someone else make the decision. Her recommendation was to sign them to a contract.

"Give us a proposal to present for approval. We need something in our hands. Over."

"I'll write up a preliminary report and a proposal. I'll email it to you today. It won't be fancy or have a lot of legal terms, but it will cover what I must have. Over and out."

Nick's hands were shaking. This was a risky gambit, but it was all he could come up with.

Without his information, they would eventually catch up with al-Zaqiri, but not before more dependents died. The press would have a field day over the revelation that the war in the Middle East had come to America. The finger pointing would be brutal, especially when it was learned that credible help had been ignored. But would it be enough to get Kiki back and keep the two of them out of jail?

Nick closed his eyes. He tried to reach out to Kiki in his mind. Don't worry, K. I'll get you out. He went to the back of the RV to check on Mohammed.

Adamson fumed, his face purple. He pounded his fist on the conference table, knocking over a glass of water. "That son of a bitch doesn't know who he's dealing with!"

Freddy smiled. "It's apparent to me that he knows quite well. Perhaps it's time to quit posturing for promotion and do something for this country."

Adamson looked like he was going to explode. He stormed out of the conference room slamming the door, endangering the glass walls.

Lieutenant Hernandez broke the dead silence. "Can we move forward around him?" He jerked his thumb at the closed door, looking at Freddy. Once again, local law enforcement was being pushed aside, but Hernandez wanted a piece of this.

"Once we have the report and proposal, I'll submit it to my boss. He'll take it to Adamson's boss. So, yeah. We will do what's right."

Sitting at the table, Nick stared hard at the computer screen, the words blurred. He had typed, retyped, edited, and revised the proposal trying to put one together that would be acceptable.

The short summary of what happened to date had been easy. He started with the murders of Kiki's family, the murders of the Albuquerque cops, and the attempted murder of Officer Mario Cava. Ricardo gave up Joaquin, who gave up Mohammed, who fingered al-Zaqiri. The assassination program was to destroy morale in the military and the American people. It brought the Middle East war to American soil. The public would react by willingly giving up their freedom and way of life for the illusion of security.

Look what they did after 9/11. He worried that it would put even more power in the hands of Homeland Security and assholes like Adamson.

What else could he do? He felt he had buddied up to the tiger to protect himself from the lion.

Nick went to the back of the motorhome to check on Mohammed and give his eyes a chance to clear. He stared at the slow waves marching across the monitor. He almost wished he were resting and isolated from this world. Almost.

Nick read over his proposal again. He and Katherine would contract with Homeland Security to hunt down the domestic members of this program. They would have access to government data systems to aid in the pursuit. They would coordinate with DHS, FBI, and other agencies needed to accomplish this end. All tapes of interrogations would be turned over.

That part was straightforward and acceptable.

The hard part would be immunity to prosecution for crimes committed in carrying out this work. Payments for services were to be made every two weeks into an overseas account in Grand Cayman. The payments were lucrative. Nick would immediately have them transferred through a series of accounts with a small part of the money returning to his bank account in the U. S.. That made the funds available, though he still had a lot of Joaquin's money. There were to be no expense invoices. Those monies were part of the payments. Less paper trail for anyone to follow.

The immunity clause would have to be signed by the President of the United States to be secure. He felt like Jack Bauer in the Fox television series *24,* only for real.

Nick did not reveal the location of Joaquin or the isolation chamber as the interrogation method. They would learn of it after the contract was signed. In the end, the contract was just a piece of paper, but he had to believe it would work. For how long? He wondered.

He printed out three copies, addressed two to Freddy Foster and signed them. He emailed the proposal to Freddy. The actual agreement might have to go through a couple of iterations, unless they were anxious to move ahead. The third copy he mailed to his family with instructions: Do not open. Keep in a safe place. Send to FOX News if he were not heard from weekly. The note would worry them, but Nick would be in touch with them more in one month than the last year.

# Chapter 29

The walls of the Andros' small office vibrated from the loud bump and grind music in the 'Gentleman's Club Showroom' next door. Describing this as a no frills office would be a gross understatement. The cheap oak paneling was splitting, the stained linoleum floor was cracked, and the desk with numerous cigarette burns had a stack of old nudie magazines replacing one leg. The hanging light swung back and forth with a mind of its own from a ceiling with holes in the acoustic panels. Smoke trailed from smoldering cigarette butts in the overflowing ashtray, adding the smell of burnt filters to the aroma of sweat and stale beer. Hashim looked at the stained couch and worried about his khaki pants.

He stared at the scarred face across the desk. One eye drifted, and one ear was partly gone. Andros Gallen had risen to head of the Charon's Children gang the hard way, by showing he was the toughest. He was also the smartest. His prowess on his bike and his ruthless control were legendary. Andros' paw engulfed Hashim's hand as they shook.

"Haven't seen ya in a while. Ya got work for us?"

"Andros, I have bad news about Niños de Noche in Albuquerque. They were hit by a rival. Joaquin, Ricardo, and two others were killed. We want to continue business there, but…" Hashim held out his hands, palms up.

"Jesus Christ!" bellowed Andros. "Who was it?"

"I am aware of only two people. I killed one, but I know nothing more. I am thinking of setting up my headquarters here in Salt Lake. I do not know who to trust in Phoenix anymore. The authorities got involved, but I managed to escape."

Through gritted teeth, Andros growled. "Okay, tell me what you know. We'll take care of it. Nobody hits Charon's Children allies and gets away with it. I'll also send my number two, Max, and a couple of his guys to Albuquerque to get them back on line. We'll run it from here."

"I do have work for you." He handed Andros a list. "You will notice that one address is near Hill Air Force Base. The other is near Las Vegas, Nellis Air Force Base. Is that a worry?"

"No prob. We'll take care of the job at Hill from here. I got a chapter in Vegas I trust. They'll do the Nellis job."

Hashim placed a kilo of heroin on the table. "What do you know of Dugway Proving Grounds?"

Andros's eyes moved from the dope to Hashim. "It's a huge Army test base. They used to test chemical weapons there, but not a lot of that going on now. The Tooele Depot was cleaned out years ago, along with most of the chem and bio stuff. It's remote. Why?"

"I just wondered." Hashim had hoped there were still chemical or biological weapons stored there that could be stolen. Perhaps not. He rose and handed Andros a phone.

"Use this phone to call me. It is to be used for our communication only. Make no other calls on it. My number is on speed dial. If you get any other calls, do not answer."

"You're bein' cautious. Any specific reason I should know about?"

"I am taking no chances. The attacks in Albuquerque, Tucson, and Phoenix are a reason to be careful."

Andros heaved himself from the cracked leather chair. "Yeah, you're right." He held up the phone. "I'll call ya on how the jobs go."

Hashim squinted in the bright sunlight after exiting the darkness of the club. These infidels were distasteful to deal with, but they were expendable. They sold their souls for drugs to poison others and make money. He regretted not being able to flood this den of disease with more heroin.

His new Lexus SUV chirped as he unlocked it. The steering wheel and seat automatically adjusted to him as he started the car. His new identity hadn't taken long to establish. The banks had been most anxious to open an account for a proper businessman with $9,000 cash. He'd opened several accounts under different names, always staying under the reportable deposit amount.

Hashim's new house was in a development near Cottonwood City, close to the interstate. The neighborhood was older and established. Behind his back yard was an open field. After moving in, he made a visit to each neighbor, introducing himself as an importer of furniture from Brazil. He assured them he could get them bargain prices.

At home, Hashim sank into the black leather recliner. His visit with Charon's Children had been good. Andros and his gang would take care of several problems for him. Mohammed was still a worry. He thumbed on the smart TV and searched the news for reports of a body found in the Picacho Peak area. Without a body, he had to assume Mohammed had been captured alive.

What group had the sniper, Katherine Russell, belonged to? How many were there? Were they police? The police had been involved in Phoenix, but what police? These were troubling questions.

Hashim pulled his laptop over, logged on and checked his email. No messages. He deposited a short encoded message of his status in his draft emails box.

Time to pray.

# Chapter 30

FBI Special Agent Freddy Foster shook her head as she looked at the report and proposal from Nick Sabino. On the walls of her office hung commendations for service, pictures of her with personages shaking her hand, handing her plaques. She believed in the rule of law, dedicated herself to it. On her speakerphone, she was in videoconference with Albert Bowers, Adamson's boss at Homeland Security, Broaderick Stephenson, her boss, and Dianne Coleman from the CIA.

Bowers looked up from his pad. "From Sabino's report, we had his activities pretty well figured out. The names of the latest men captured prove an international connection through Mexico to the Middle East, most specifically Afghanistan. His offer to coordinate on the capture of Hashim al-Zaqiri tells me he doesn't have confidence he can do it alone."

"I like his honest assessment of his own capabilities," said Freddy.

"We will eventually find al-Zaqiri," stated Coleman.

Maybe you could use some humble and honest self-assessment yourself, thought Freddy.

"As you can see, Nick signed the contract," said Freddy. "I have problems with any agreement that grants immunity for crimes that may be committed even in the act of saving others. Nick Sabino and Katherine Russell committed several serious crimes, including kidnapping and murder."

Unlike many in Washington and the current administration, Freddy did not believe the ends justified the means. That principle put them on the same level as those they fought. "I cannot accept this agreement." In her heart, she saw no acceptable alternative, but she wanted to voice the position of moral high ground.

"Freddy, the FBI has gained invaluable information on the drug distribution system and OMGs. Surely, you can see the value in this. I have reservations, but think it should go forward," said Stephenson.

"Using his information allows us to move forward on al-Zaqiri. The Department of Homeland Security can keep a tight leash on Nick Sabino and Katherine Russell," said Bowers. "We need to move quickly, follow the trail of this organization back to the source. Sabino and

Russell seem to have the means of getting information vital to that effort."

"I agree," said Stephenson, "but we must insist on close oversight." Bowers was nodding.

Oversight for what? wondered Freddy. These were actions both of the other agencies condoned and used at times. This was like putting a drug addict in charge of the pharmacy.

"Whatever methods these two used to extract information, they saved lives," said Bowers. "Their killing of the two attackers in Tucson was justified self-defense."

Freddy believed killing of the two gang-bangers, Ricardo and Joaquin, was not – it was murder.

"I recommend that each crime be judged on the evidence," she offered. "In the case of Ricardo de Silva, no evidence was found at the scene of the body. There may be some at the scene of the murder, wherever that is. When the body of Joaquin de Silva is found, we might have evidence linking his death to Nick and Katherine." Part of her hoped not. "At that point, we decide about immunity."

Dianne Coleman spoke up. "The interrogation methods were quite interesting. Ricardo de Silva showed no signs of trauma or torture. The autopsy revealed an embolism stopped his heart, a rather peaceful way to go.

"There were IV sites. If Sabino and Russell used drugs to question him, we need to learn more. CIA interrogations with medications have proven unreliable. The autopsy showed a whole spectrum of drugs – stimulants, depressants, lysergic acid dithalomide, curanine, and others we haven't identified yet."

Bowers piped up. "Yet, they got critical information, and they did so quickly."

Homeland Security and the CIA were both clamoring to learn more. Freddy had no doubt the case of Joaquin would be the same MO as with Ricardo.

"Nick's captive has information crucial in countering international terrorism. That is critical to CIA efforts overseas," added Coleman. "When our allies learn about this military dependent murder program, they will be screaming for information. Based on performance, Nick is more adept at getting it than anyone else. Our allies will not be squeamish about how we get the information."

Freddy knew this would mean letting Nick and Katherine continue their examination using whatever methods they employed.

"As to the woman, Katherine Russell," continued Coleman, "she is the only hold we have on Sabino."

"But she is also a liability," argues Freddy. "If Sabino has a press package, the federal government holding an Afghanistan war hero will not play well. Veterans could be quite vocal about her captivity, especially if she was on the hunt for the murderers of her family, something LEOs got nowhere on. Bringing that out will reveal the terrorist program against military dependents, something better released in a controlled manner. It will come out; there is no doubt of that. Anybody looking at the murder statistics can correlate with military deaths, but it will be better released by the government with a solution."

Freddy had said her piece. She was sure an agreement would be reached with Nick. A nagging little voice in the back of her mind whispered it might be a deal with the devil.

# Chapter 31

The room Kiki was in resembled a hospital room. It had monitors on the wall and oxygen plug-ins, but it didn't feel right. The door was closed, something most hospitals only did when private procedures were taking place. She heard no announcements, another thing incessant in most hospitals. When she had gone to the bathroom, she tried the door. It was locked. The window was frosted security glass with wires forming a diamond pattern. She was definitely a prisoner. She felt fine, except for the persistent headache, but there was no reason to let them know that. The door opened.

"Get dressed, Mrs. Russell. You're moving to other quarters. Our doctors assure us you are healthy enough for a trip."

Kiki eyed the stocky matron standing at the foot of the bed. "Where am I going?"

"Someplace safe. Now get dressed." She scowled, threw gray scrubs on the bed, crossed her arms, and glared.

Safe for whom, wondered Kiki. Nick, I sure could use you and the medevac right now. The shackles were a shock.

Kiki glanced at the clear blue sliver of sky as they went through the double doors. She saw no visible markings on the ambulance as they climbed into the back. Kiki's stomach fluttered. She felt as if she were in a movie, and an unpleasant scene was about to begin.

The ambulance stopped. She heard voices. They started moving again. In the view through the back window, she saw a military gate. The trip was short, with little traffic on the road behind them. Two armed men in unfamiliar black uniforms opened the ambulance door. Kiki looked at a small jet parked inside a hangar.

This was getting worse. "Where are you taking me?" she asked. Her question was ignored as they climbed the steps and entered. The matron walked her through the aisle to the bathroom. It was tight with the door open, barely enough room to do her business.

The matron escorted her back to a seat and locked her shackles to a loop on the floor under the seat. After testing the chain with a shake, the matron turned and left, along with the two men in black. Nobody else was in the cabin.

Takeoff without a fasten seatbelts warning seemed strange. She got no beverage service. The windows were blanked, she couldn't see out. She dozed.

The clunk of the landing gear extending awoke her. How many hours had it been? The landing was hard, and not too soon for Kiki.

The door opened and a different rough-faced woman in gray coveralls entered. She unlocked Kiki and walked her back to the bathroom. Thank God, thought Kiki. Door or no door, she didn't care.

Descending the steps, the matron kept a firm grip on her arm. They were in another hangar, but it was warm and humid. Where were they? She shuffled to a waiting van.

Kiki looked out through the back, acutely aware of the matron's hand on her arm. What lights she saw were subdued, but the chain-link fences with razor wire on top gave her a start. A light flashed green and white atop a tower. It was an airport, but where? This reminded her of the POW camps in Afghanistan. With rising dread, the name Guantanamo popped into her head.

"You can't do this to me." She was shoved through a steel framed door, tripping over the shackles. The cell had concrete walls and a bare concrete floor. A steel frame bed was anchored to the floor, a combination stainless steel sink and toilet on one wall. The light was built into a concrete ceiling. The steel door clanged shut behind her.

"Put your hands through the window," came a gruff voice. The first words she'd heard since the hospital.

She did so, and a hand unlocked her bracelets. A steel plate slid shut.

"Now turn around and put your heels against the door."

Kiki got the idea and complied. A plate near the floor slid open and her shackles were unlocked. "Where am I?" she shouted. Her question echoed to silence. God, she was thirsty. At the sink, she cupped her hands under the faucet, pushing a small lever. She drank despite the vile smell and taste of the water. The light went out.

In the pitch black, she felt her way to the bed. No sheets, no pillow, just a straw mat. She closed her eyes as tears streamed out. She bit her lip. Kiki would not give them the satisfaction of hearing her sobs.

# Chapter 32

Freddy assessed the task force. Was it really that? She didn't know, but the number of attendees had increased. Physically present in Freddy's office were Tucson Police Lieutenant Hernandez; Homeland Security Assistant Director Albert Bowers; and CIA Agent Dianne Coleman. Other members were teleconferencing.

"Nick, we have a counter proposal for you," said Dianne Coleman. "You and Mrs. Russell will be pardoned for all past crimes that you admit. You start with clean slates. We will free her in return for Mohammed al-Harabi. You will become contractors. You will be responsible for any crimes committed in the future. We will oversee your actions, including your interrogations. You will act with our prior approval. Over."

This proposal was hammered out despite my objections, thought Freddy. Though of questionable legality, it was fair.

Nick listened. Sighing, he knew this was where they would end up. It was reasonable. "Who would we work directly under?" he asked. "Over."

"You answer to me," stated Freddy. "That means you are working for the FBI. We will coordinate with DHS, CIA, and the locals. Department of Justice oversees us. Over."

"Are the locals in agreement with this? Over," asked Nick.

Lieutenant Hernandez spoke, "We haven't forgotten you saved the life of one of ours and would have done so in Albuquerque, given the chance. We haven't found Joaquin de Silva and have more important things on our plates. Nobody has reported him missing. We therefore cannot open a case. We're good with it. Over."

Good, thought Nick. That was off his plate.

"Before I come in, I will finish questioning Mohammed. You can have him afterward. I will share the tapes with you. Katherine would help, but I understand we have to do an exchange. You'll get Mohammed when I'm finished. I'll have him ready for you in two days. Over."

"Where will the exchange take place? Over," asked Freddy.

"I'll know after I finish with Mohammed. Over."

"I'm emailing you the agreement with these stipulations. Sign it and mail it back. Tell us where you want her. Over," said Freddy.

"I'll let you know when I mail the contract. Over."

"What about Hashim? What are you going to do? Over," asked Freddy

"Once I locate him, Kiki and I will do a recon. We'll get back to you to formulate a plan. Over."

"We have assets to help find him. We need to team up on this. Don't try this alone. You fucked it up once and look where it got you. Over," said Coleman.

Nick was quiet. She was right, but it stung. Something in Coleman's voice made Nick uneasy, but he had no choice. This was the only plan.

"We want Mohammed, and we want al-Zaqiri. Over."

"You'll get Mohammed after I've questioned him. My methods are more effective than yours. Over."

"Remember, you will be accountable for any crimes you commit. That includes torture. Over," said Freddy.

"I understand what must be done. Over and out."

Nick understood all right. To prosecute him for torture, they would have to have evidence. The only witness would be unable to testify. There would be no marks on Mohammed to prove torture. He had to finish questioning him alone.

Nick sensed there was something Mohammed held back. He also needed more leads on Hashim's whereabouts. In the back of the motorhome, he stared at the isolation chamber. He made adjustments to the IV drips. The monitors showed Mohammed's consciousness level rising.

*"Mohammed, your song of your life is going well, but there are parts you have left out. Your song must be complete for you to enter Paradise."*

Nick watched the brainwave monitors. The activity level rose, but it was not panic. He was confused by the words that formed in his mind. "What have I left out?"

*"You were going to serve me by attacking the infidels. Who was helping you?"*

"It was Hashim. He was going to a place called Salt Lake City so I could meet the leader of Charon's Children. They would assist me in killing the infidels and demoralizing those troops fighting us. We were to bring our fight for you to the soil of the Great Satan, America."

*"Who gave you and Hashim directions?"*

Nick could see Mohammed's pulse rate rise, his breathing become more rapid on the monitors. Something was agitating him. A resonate voice, unaccented and not Mohammed's, echoed from the isolation chamber in a smooth whisper.

**"Hello, Nicholas Sabino. The question you have asked Mohammed, he cannot answer. The directions came from me. I made those decisions."**

The voice hung in the air. Nick froze, his mouth fell open. He was stunned. Where did this come from? Had he tapped into some second persona of Mohammed's? His mind raced. It had to be a second personality. But, how did he know Nick's name? He strained to remember if there was any way Mohammed could know that. This was coming from Mohammed, wasn't it? Where else?

"Who are you?"

**"You may call me the Director,"** the voice like sandpaper sheets rubbed together.

"The Director? The director of what? What is your name?"

***"You humans have a need to assign a name. Just call me the Director."***

This had to be a deep-rooted personality of Mohammed. He probably wasn't even aware of it. How interesting. "What do you direct?"

***"At this very instant, I am within Mohammed speaking to you. But that changes."***

A shiver crawled down Nick's spine. Was something really within Mohammed? He didn't like the alternative. He searched within himself. "I don't understand. Can you explain?"

The voice was low, raspy. ***"The best explanation you could understand would be that I am a spirit, an essence, if you will. I enter minds through contact. That contact can be physical, or through communication."***

"Communication? You mean verbal?"

*"Verbal, electronic, written, it matters not. It is the connection between two minds upon which I travel. I direct minds in their visions."*

"What do you mean 'direct'? Do you control people?" Nick's mind was a jumble. This had to be coming from Mohammed, but how?

*"I do not control. I influence."*

Nick felt a touch of panic. Was his mind going off the rails? Too long without sleep, too much worry? "Explain. I do not understand. I don't believe you."

*"I will cite an example with which you are familiar. When Katherine thought about Ricardo dying, I brought to her mind the image of her family being murdered. It was a detailed scene. Those images evoked shock, then hatred. That hatred grew within her, obscuring all else. She wanted him to suffer horribly. You saw it in her."*

The memory of Kiki staring at the isolation chamber, hatred boiling out of her, rose in his mind. Only two people were there, at least only two conscious people. Oh God! What was happening to him?

"Why would you do that?"

***"I live on human emotion. It is my sustenance. I especially like the tastes of hatred and fear. The stronger the emotion, the stronger I become."***

Was this coming from himself, his psyche? "You direct them to violence?" Nick asked, alarm in his voice.

***"It's not that simple. First comes hatred. I inject images and ideas to build hatred. Fear works well to initiate action. Hatred impels fear, which pushes hatred. Violence erupts from this mix. And builds more hatred and fear. It's delicious."***

"How many do you direct?"

***"Oh, not that many, but those I direct are in charge. They do most of the work for me. Once the violence starts, it spreads***

*amidst rising hatred and fear. It is contagious. Hatred and fear are the emotions I want. I can get them from anyone. The battlefield is a feast."*

This had to be a hallucination. Too much stress, like battlefield stress.

"You're not real!"

*"Nicholas, who are you trying to convince? Your fear is showing."*

Nick felt doubt, doubt that the voice was real, doubt that it was a hallucination. If it was not real, he was cracking up. What Mohammed said, Nick's name, about Kiki, he could not have known. If it was real, what was it?

"Who are you?" he screamed.

*"I told you who I am. You choose not to accept."*

"If you're real, if you're what you say you are, you've invaded Mohammed's mind. By your own words, you transfer through communication, like an infection. You're like a disease, a virus!" shouted Nick. He heard laughter. "You're a mental virus!"

*"Ha ha! That is an apt description. I like it."*

Worry shook him. "Will I get infected?"

*"Oh, Nicholas. You already are. I can taste your fear. Fear of yourself has a wonderful tang."*

Nick stumbled from the back room. Laughter followed him out.

Infected! What did that mean? He had to calm down, get hold on his emotions. Nick took a deep breath. He willed himself not to feel anything.

*"Not even for Ricardo and Joaquin?"*

That wasn't from Mohammed, from the speakers in the isolation Chamber. It was in his head! Where did that thought come from? Laughter echoed in his mind.

*"What did you feel for them?"*

He hated them! They killed K's family, they hurt Kiki. There was no remorse over their deaths, only satisfaction. He held the same hatred for Mohammed and Hashim. He'd not hesitate to kill them too. He stopped. Was this the infection? What about fear of this 'essence'? Did that count?

**"You're learning, Nick. Fear of me will lead to hatred, which will make me stronger. Difficult, is it not?"**

Nick burst from the motorhome, gasping. The stark red rocks and sheer cliffs of Zion National Park surrounded him. He stared, spinning around, willing himself not to think. When his legs weakened, he sat on a rock at the edge of the parking lot. He had to put this aside for now. He had things to do. Focus, he told himself. He had the information to get started. First and foremost was to get Kiki back.

# Chapter 33

Andros pulled his feet off the desk to answer the phone. "Yeah?"

"Andros, we're here, man, in Albuquerque. Got us a place, checked out Joaquin's house."

Andros sat up, suddenly attentive.

"Hey, Max, anythin' at the house?"

"No sign of life, like he just disappeared. There's pigs watching it off and on. We went to his club and asked for him. Nobody knew anything, hadn't heard from him in days. When he left, all he told them was he would be back. Didn't happen. That place is gonna fall apart without a manager. Man, we're going to have to start from scratch. You got any contacts?"

"Yeah, Max. I got names. Start at his club, The Bandit. You're now the manager. Any resistance, you handle it. Pull in the street guys. Tell 'em you'll have a re-up in a day or two. Hold a meeting with the rest of the Niños. Tell 'em you're settin' things up. You'll be their supplier. Explain it's just until Joaquin gets back.

"I'll get word to Charon's Children in Mexico to get the supply set up. I'll tell 'em who you are, and when you'll be there for a pickup.

"Use that key of H to get in. Don't step on it too hard. We wanna build a rep for quality. I'll get the regular stuff flowin' to ya."

"What about the contract work? You got anything for us?" asked Max.

"We did the one here and the one in Vegas. The man hasn't been back to me on any others. I'll let him know we're ready for business in New Mexico and Arizona again. Call me in a day or two."

Nick was scrolling news when the headline came on:

### *Military wife and four children brutally murdered in Layton, Utah.*

*Kaitlan Smith, wife of Air Force Captain Dillon Smith, was found dead inside her Layton, Utah home when neighbors hadn't seen her or the children for a day. Their four children, ages two, three, five, and seven were also found dead in the house. In an act of pure brutality, all were beheaded.*

Oh, shit! Nick continued reading the details. Another headline caught his attention:

*Vicious murder of woman and her three children in East Las Vegas.*
*The body of Maureen Henley, wife of Air Force Specialist Fifth Class Robert Henley, and their three children ere found in their east Las Vegas home. All four victims were beheaded. No motive has been established...*

Christ! He felt responsible. Was this because they had captured Mohammed or was it a continuation of the terrorism program? It didn't matter. He and K had missed Hashim. Mohammed said that operations would be expanding into Nevada and Utah. That's where Hashim had gone, where Nick was heading. It was time to call

Freddy. He shut down his computer and pulled out his phone. From the motorhome window he looked out at the rest stop in Springville, Utah. It was beautiful country.

The shortwave hissed at him. He pressed the send button. "Freddy, you there? Over."

"Yeah, we're here. It's the same team as before. After the latest murders hit the news, we went into emergency meeting. We have to move on this now. Where are you? Over."

"Heading north. I signed your version of the contract. Did you get it? Over."

"Yeah," snapped Dianne Coleman. "Everything is good to go. Can we quit with this Mickey Mouse communication system crap now? Over."

"Okay. Meet me at the Salt Lake City FBI office tomorrow at four. Bring Kiki. I'll have Mohammed. You'll need an ambulance to move him. We have a lot to discuss and face-to-face will be best." Nick's heart sped up. His world had become a rollercoaster going "click-click-click" as it approached the top of the first drop. He took a deep breath.

"In the meantime" directed Nick, "set up surveillance on the Charon's Children headquarters in Salt Lake. I'm sure you already know where it is. Put taps on the phones. Hashim is in that area and Charon's Children are his contractors. Look into the murders in Layton and Las Vegas with an eye toward Charon's Children as the perps. Mohammed said they would be expanding into those areas. See you tomorrow. Over and out." He trembled, feeling like he'd just jumped into the jaws of the whale and faith was all he had to keep him safe.

Freddy looked at those gathered in her office. "I'll notify the Salt Lake FBI office to get with local law enforcement so we can start our surveillance." She addressed Agent Bowers. "HSD has the budget. How about tasking a drone for us?"

He nodded. "I'll get one."

Freddy continued. "We suspected these latest murders were the work of Hashim, but the press has sniffed out that something is afoot. We are on a timeline to take care of this before they find out enough to go national. Within a day, two at the most, murders related to military dependents will become the headline. Reporters will give legs to the story with rabid ferocity."

All three of the federal agents, FBI, CIA, and HSD bowed their shoulders picturing themselves warding off the questions from their superiors. This was about to resemble a monkey trying to fuck a football. They would be the footballs. They needed to move fast while they still could.

After the last session with Mohammed, Nick had been dreading another. Yet, he had to find everything out. He made a reservation at the KOA near American Fork. It would be less than an hour drive into Salt Lake from there.

He struggled to control his fear of the 'virus'. Nick didn't like the name Director but didn't know what else to call it. He truly believed that fear would only feed it. Apprehension was a word that was inadequate for his feelings. Nonetheless, he had to go back inside Mohammed's mind – for the last time.

# Chapter 34

The rattle of the key and the clang of the door announced that Kiki had visitors. These were the first since her arrival. How long? She had no way to tell time. The light came on. She blinked while her eyes adjusted.

"Wake up, Mrs. Russell. Traveling day for you. Put these on," said the buff matron. She tossed the plastic grocery bag on the bed.

Squinting through the glare, Kiki looked into the hard pock-marked face above. The bag revealed a pair of jeans and a man's button-up shirt. Where were they taking her now? As she dressed, the woman stared above her at the wall, eyes never wavering.

Her questioning had been relentless. In her case, the torture was hour upon hour of interrogation in stark rooms under harsh lights. Her only response was "Lawyer."

The matron opened the door, indicating Kiki was to leave her cell. No shackles this time. That was a good sign. Exiting the building, she was surprised to find it was night. Her time reference was totally screwed up. This time, a car took her to the airport. Outside, the chain-link fences with barbed wire glinted in glaring lights. The car drove into a hangar and pulled up next to a small jet, engines idling. The matron pointed to the open hatch.

Nobody else was on the plane. Before she was seated, the plane was rolling. Kiki settled into a seat and buckled the belt. For the first time since she was taken prisoner, she relaxed. They had questioned her, but nothing like the interrogations of the other prisoners. Why? Was it because she wasn't a terrorist? Was it because of her time in Afghanistan? Why were they letting her go now? The questions bounced around in her head. The roar of the engines pushed them into a recess of her mind as, like all soldiers, she took advantage of the opportunity to sleep.

With a shiver, Nick brought Mohammed back to consciousness straining to hear any voice other than Mohammed's.

*"You finished the song of your life. Your early years formed you into my servant, the carrier of my message, guardian of the faithful. My servant, Hashim, is now in the next location with the hired infidels ready to continue. Sing of that."*

Nick listened as Mohammed told of the voyage aboard the luxury yacht to western Mexico, the road trip to Chihuahua, his drive north to Phoenix. He told of Hashim and the network using the Outlaw Motorcycle Gang, Charon's Children. They had chapters in Las Vegas, Albuquerque, Phoenix, and Salt Lake City, acting as distributors for the Middle Eastern heroin. They were the contract killers sapping the will of the American military fighters. It was the last episode of Mohammed's life.

Nick looked at the isolation chamber, wishing he could send Mohammed to meet Allah for real. His agreement was to turn him over to Freddy and the FBI. It would be interesting to see what they ended up with in the deal. Nick knew Mohammed believed he was dead, awaiting entry into Paradise. What would happen when he learned he would have to die again? Worse, he would realize the song of his life was his ultimate betrayal.

*"Nicely done, Nicholas. I will enjoy Mohammed's return to 'life' immensely. It will be a unique combination of flavors. And I will be watching you."*

Nick froze. That voice was back. It was in his head! He put his hands over his ears as if to ward off the words. I'm going crazy! This isn't real.

*"I'm real and you know it."*

"Get out!" he screamed. He spun, wildly.

*"Nicholas, you cannot wish me away any more than you can wish away the flu. As a virus finds fertile ground in living cells, I like your mind."*

Nick stood still, shuddering. He took deep breaths trying to calm himself. Panic started to rise again. He squashed it back down. He forced himself to believe it was another entity and not his own hallucination. "Why have you revealed yourself to me? Are you just one or are there more of you?"

*"I like you, Nicholas. And your awareness of me makes this even more delicious. You cannot help yourself. You will commit violence. And you are afraid of that."*

"Are you the only essence feeding on me, on people?"

*"I am many more than one, with many appetites."*

"Are there some of you who aren't evil?"

*"Evil is such a subjective term. We feed on the whole spectrum of human emotions. We influence human minds to enhance those emotions. War and terrorism elicit such intense emotion. I prefer the hot spicy flavor of hatred and the sour taste of fear."*

"Are there others of you who like happiness?"

*"Happiness is sweet, fresh, but it rarely lasts long. It is not as intense as hatred."*

"What about love?"

*"It is not a taste I like, too sweet, but yes, others like that flavor."*

"Love between mates, family, fellow humans, brothers and sisters. Love as taught by religions."

*"Yes, others thrive on those flavors, though we both feed at the trough of religions."*

"Can we escape you?"

*"Can a fish escape the sea?"*

Nick had to think this over. "Is there any way for me to be alone, away from you?"

*"We are a part of you. There is no 'away'."*

# Chapter 35

Nick circled the block twice, not just out of habit. He was still shaken by his last encounter with the thing, the director. He snapped back. Have to focus, he told himself. Get Kiki back. Nothing seemed amiss, but he wouldn't see it if there was. His cell phone was connected.

"Freddy, I'm pulling into the parking lot now. I'll park next to the ambulance. Mohammed's sedated."

Freddy met Nick at the garage elevator door. "A pleasure to meet you at last." She held out her hand. "How long will he be out?" she asked, nodding toward Mohammed.

Nick was surprised by this elfin woman with the bright eyes. He had pictured her much larger. She had a strong grip.

"Several hours, but he may be in bad shape when he wakes up. You'll need a doctor and a psychiatrist. Physically, he hasn't been touched."

Freddy looked at the man lying in the back of the van, signaled for the ambulance attendants to bring the gurney. She glanced around the inside of the van.

"Where's Kiki?" asked Nick.

"She's upstairs waiting for us."

Relief filled Nick. He had her back. Almost.

Freddy led him up a flight of stairs and down a hallway. Outside a door, she paused and glanced at Nick. Stepping, back, she guided him in.

Nick barely had time to react as Kiki launched herself into his arms. God, she felt good.

"Oh, Nick. There were times I didn't think I'd see you again."

Nick unpeeled her arms. "I never doubted it. There are things we have to do before we can leave." Nick looked at the assembled agents and police. "I need to speak to Katherine before we bring her up to date. Freddy, is there an office we can use?"

The local FBI chief rose. "Follow me. You can use my office."

Nick faced Kiki, their knees touching. He took her hands in his. "I've had to make some deals to get you out and to get help. The short version is that we are now contractors to the FBI. We'll turn over all the interview tapes and Mohammed. Mohammed was the man with Hashim. You tased him. I've milked him dry. There wasn't enough to lead directly to Hashim, but with local and fed help, we'll catch him." Nick saw a hard look pass over Kiki's face at the mention of Hashim. He squeezed her hand to reassure her.

"Our past misdeeds are pardoned, but not the future ones. We'll have to get an okay before we capture, interrogate, or off anyone. We'll have to turn anyone we take over to them. All of this is spelled out in the contract. On the reality side, our interrogations are better than theirs, so they will give us the okay." Kiki nodded her agreement.

"As to turning over people, I honestly think they'll get nothing. Mohammed truly believes he is dead. His awakening to a real world will break his mind. He will choose to retreat into the belief he is dead. Mohammed is the highest baddie we've captured. He is here to take over the assassination program so Hashim can go to other parts of the country. Mohammed was sent from their headquarters in Afghanistan."

"We're going to stop them, Nick. We have to," exclaimed Kiki.

He nodded. "K, I also came across something else with Mohammed, but we'll go into that later. I edited those particular tapes. You'll see why. Sorry to have to spring this on you so quickly. Any questions?"

"It's a lot to assimilate, Nick. I trust you. I have to. And thanks for getting me out. I haven't said that yet."

He put his hand on her shoulder. "We'll be okay. Look, just go with me on this. I'll fill you in when we're alone. I'll want to hear what happened to you, too. We need to get back to the conference room." He rose, giving Kiki a hand up.


Nick and Kiki took the two empty seats at the table.

"Mrs. Russell, Katherine, may I call you Katherine?" asked Freddy.

Kiki nodded.

"Katherine, Nick, I'll introduce you. I'm Special Agent Freddy Foster with the FBI. This is Chief Zack Young of the Salt Lake City police." The medium height slender man stood. He shook both Nick's and Kiki's hands.

"Next to him is Special Agent David Wilson of the local FBI office." Wilson was the only non-white at the table. He towered over Kiki as he shook her hand. "Next to him is Albert Bowers of Homeland Security." The man was easily the tallest man in the room. He brushed wisps of white hair from his forehead and held out his hand.

"I'd also like to introduce you to Dianne Coleman with the Central Intelligence Agency."

The attractive medium-height woman stood. She had midnight hair cut in a pageboy. She nodded, holding out her hand, first to Kiki then to Nick. "Mrs. Russell, your reputation in Afghanistan is legendary. We believe your effectiveness is what led to this situation and your presence here.

"Nick, I've been briefed on what you and Kiki, is it all right to call you that?" Kiki nodded, "have accomplished. Let us make no mistake here. We have contracted with you because, as independents, you do the things we are forbidden from doing. Yet we need you desperately."

"I gather that means you'll cut us loose and let us hang if we're caught," said Nick.

"Politics is an ugly game," said Bowers. They looked at him. He was almost gaunt. "First off, I'd like to apologize for Agent Adamson's behavior. We're trying to develop his diplomatic skills, convince him that terrorists are the enemy, all others are allies. We have to thank you for what you've done." He held up a hand. "Yeah, I know I don't sound like a bureaucrat. The only reason I'm still around is my results speak louder than my lack of bureaucratic acumen. So, let's cut to the chase. What do you have for us?"

Nick handed him the tapes of Ricardo's, Joaquin's and Mohammed's (edited to remove conversations with the director) interviews. "These are extensive, with detailed information. In essence, we have milked them dry. Do not be surprised if Mohammed yields nothing."

"We would like you to help our interrogators learn your techniques," said Dianne.

"Why not remain ignorant and let us contractors interrogate for you? It protects you," said Kiki, smiling. She knew they were being set up to take a hard fall if anything went wrong. They would have observers, but not agents.

Christ, she learned this game fast, Nick thought.

"We would like our observers present," answered Dianne.

"To the interviews, certainly," said Nick.

"What do you need from us?" asked Bowers.

"I need everything you've got on Charon's Children," said Nick.

Everybody at the table looked at Chief Zack Young. He was tapping on his tablet. "It's being sent to you now. They're a particularly nasty group of bikers distributing meth through our fair land. We bust them when we get enough cause to prosecute. The local chapter leader is Andros Galen. His specifics are in the file. He's a nasty piece of work, no conscience, does the work because he likes it. Recently they've expanded from meth to heroin.

"A witness in the recent murders in Layton placed a couple of motorcycles in the area at the time. Charon's Children are high on the suspect list. We have surveillance cameras on his headquarters and his home."

"Well done, Chief," said Kiki. "Nick, what do we need?" She turned toward him.

God, she hadn't lost a beat, thought Nick. It's like she's back in Afghanistan, planning a mission.

"We need surveillance tapes of home and business over the last three days. We also want the telephone records of all the phones you are monitoring. I'll let you know after that."

Chief Young looked around the table. "Agent Foster, Agent Bowman, You've shared little information with me regarding Katherine and Nick and their part in this operation. Why do you need them as contractors?"

"Chief Young, this operation is classified," said Bowman. "I'm not one to throw around the weight of the Department of Homeland Security lightly, but in this case, the fewer people who know the better. I'm asking for your cooperation."

Chief Young understood that the politely worded request was anything but. "I'm not comfortable sharing confidential information on an open investigation with civilians."

"Fine," said Freddy. "Give us the information. We'll see that it is properly distributed. If you're uncomfortable with how we use it, you may leave the room. What happens here is strictly confidential. No information may leave this room and those attending can say nothing."

The chief remained sitting. Too interesting a case, isn't it chief, thought Freddy.

"Kiki, Nick, we'll bring you into the information loop. You'll get whatever we have," Freddy said. The chief would not be sitting in on the interrogation sessions, thought Freddy.

# Chapter 36

On the drive back to Spanish Fork, Nick told Kiki what he'd seen after she tased Mohammed.

"After Hashim forced you into the car, I secured Mohammed and followed in the van. I couldn't get you back from Hashim alive, so I called the cops." He glanced at her for a reaction, but she was immobile.

"They spotted Hashim's car and followed it to the house. As they were preparing for an assault and rescue, you burst through the garage door in the car. The house blew right after that. I watched the cops load you into an ambulance." Nick looked at Kiki again. "K, I didn't know what to do. I felt helpless."

Kiki sat silently, staring out of the car, her lips a thin line.

"I disappeared from the scene, knowing if they had me, neither of us would be free again. Back at the RV park, I interrogated Mohammed, learned more about Hashim." Nick's hands tightened on the steering wheel, remembering the frustration he'd felt. "I had to get more information. From what Mohammed said, I was sure Hashim was headed for Salt Lake City." Nick saw Kiki's jaw tighten.

"I started talking with the cops, putting together a plan to get you back. Of course, they were insistent I turn myself in, but that wasn't going to happen until I had a deal." Pausing, he looked over at her. "It's the best I could do. We get to keep hunting these slime-balls and use the authorities' resources."

"What of our capture and interrogation of these guys? They might charge us with kidnapping and torture," exclaimed Kiki.

"The immunity covers the past. Future captures and interrogations will be a concern. You and I are going to review the Charon's Children surveillance tapes looking for Hashim. We're the only ones who have seen his face. Either Andros or Hashim will have to be taken for interrogation. There will be agents with us for the capture. That makes it legal. We'll prep and set up the isolation chamber alone. An agent cannot take part because that could be considered illegal. Agents will have video presence when we start questioning. They can give us questions to ask and view the questioning to assure that torture isn't taking place. All they'll see is the outside of the IC.

When we're done, we'll turn everything over to them."

Kiki looked at Nick. "I don't know where our original plan was going to lead, but this wasn't it." She shook her head, took a deep breath. "Nick, this is partly my fault. I didn't plan a deep enough extraction from this mission. I didn't consider the endgame. All I wanted to do was kill these bastards," she spat.

"I know," confirmed Nick. "We have to go with this for now, keeping records of everything. Any attempt to prosecute us, and it goes to the press. It's the only protection we have."

"I guess it's the best we could hope for," said Kiki. "I had time to think while they had me. It took effort not to transfer my hatred to them. They didn't play hardball with me. I was grateful for that. My drive to rid the world of these bad guys hasn't diminished. We both want the same thing."

Nick was relieved they were back on the same page. "For now, that's true." He shook his head. "The problem is I still don't see a good exit strategy."

Entering the motorhome, Kiki let out a huge sigh. Humble as it was, this was home. Nick and Kiki held onto each other in an embrace like castaways clinging to driftwood. Kiki felt warmth and security in his arms. Slowly, she allowed the shield she had erected to melt away.

"Nick, I wasn't sure I'd get out." Her voice trembled. A shudder passed through her.

"K, I'd die before giving up." He kissed her on the forehead, but she tipped her head back. He sought her lips. The kiss lasted a long time.

She pushed back from him. "I'm still a little overwhelmed going from a prisoner back to a hunter so quickly. I'm sure of one thing, I'm starving for you, Nick, but let's fix dinner first. The food at Guantanamo was barely edible."

The high-end canned soup and fresh salad were quick and easy. Pushing her plate away, Kiki burped, laughed, and looked at Nick. "Filled me up."

Nick nodded in agreement.

"K, while I was questioning Mohammed, a strange thing happened. I want you to listen to the unedited tapes."

# Chapter 37

Max Bolger was working hard to take over the show club and drug operations of Niños de Noche. The initial kilo of heroin was half gone. He also needed a re-up on meth. The club was an easy takeover. Nobody objected when he said they were the new temporary managers. The girls didn't care as long as they were working. Being 'temporary' there wasn't the usual jostling for favors. Joaquin would bring everything back to normal, they assumed.

Time to call Andros.

"Hey, Max, how's it goin'?"

"I took over management of the club and held a meeting with Niños."

"You get any trouble?"

"Nah. Most of them didn't even notice Joaquin was gone, so I said he was on a little vacation." He chuckled. "They accepted that. Some asked about why Charon's Children sent people down. 'Because that's what Joaquin wanted,' I told them. It quieted them for now."

"Fucking good deal. I'm expanding."

You're expanding? thought Max. It's my ass down here. "I'm going to need more soldiers when they realize Joaquin isn't coming back."

"Yeah, I'll get you some help 'til you learn what's what and who the players are."

"I also need product. Half of the brick we brought is gone. I haven't found where Joaquin kept his stash of meth, so I need that and weed. Can you start our supply out of Juarez?"

"I'll call La Sombra."

"Good, because the longer we have a shortage, the more it encourages the competition. Don't want that."

"The man may have a job there."

"No problem. I can do it with Li'l Boy. Get me the name and address."

"Call you back about supply."

Max stared at the phone. He wanted Albuquerque. Once he had supply going and brought everybody in line, he could move out from under Andros' thumb.

Andros picked up La Sombra's phone and punched in his number from memory. "Albuquerque's started again. We're going to need a resupply."

Hashim's smooth voice answered. "Very good. I'll meet you in the parking lot for Swinging Bridge Creek. It's just south of Timpanogos Cave National Monument on route 92."

"Yeah, I know where it is. What time?"

"Three-o'clock this afternoon."

"Right."

"I'll bring you another brick to keep you going. I'll set up delivery from Juarez for your Albuquerque group. In return, I have names in El Paso for your people."

"I thought you might. We're ready."

"See you at three."

Hashim smiled to himself. The loss of the Albuquerque gang had hardly been a problem. Less than a week, and they were back up and running.

He logged onto his email to update them and set up the pipeline to the new Albuquerque gang.


The ring of Freddy's phone tore her attention from the pile of paperwork on her desk. "Agent Foster, we picked up a call on Andros' phone to his second in command. It sounds like they've established themselves in Albuquerque.

They were asking Andros for a re-up," said Special Agent David Wilson.

"Thanks, Dave. We'll put a drone on Charon's Children headquarters. We might catch him meeting Hashim."

"Galen will be the one on the yellow chopper with flames on the tank," offered Wilson.

"Thanks for the ID. I'll let you know what we've got."

Freddy called the drone surveillance team to task them.

An hour later, Andros' bar was in the crosshairs of the viewer showing on her monitor. Comings and goings were noted, license plates recorded. It was routine traffic. Freddy paid little attention until her link pinged. She stared at the picture on the monitor as a helmeted figure astraddle the yellow chopper emerged from the attached garage.

Freddy called her surveillance team. "Stay on him." She brought in ground units to follow him, switching off so he wouldn't make them. If the opportunity arose, they'd take Hashim.

She called Nick.

In the motorhome, he answered. "We have Andros under a drone. We think he's meeting

Hashim. Think you can ID him if I tie you into the visual? If we can, we'll take him."

"Maybe. Be careful," admonished Nick. "He may off himself if he thinks he's going to be captured. We need him alive."

"Right, okay. We'll immobilize him first. Makes it a lot tougher. Thanks for the warning."

On her monitor, the bike pulled into a parking lot on the Alpine Loop. It was wooded, not fully visible from the air. They dare not bring the drone lower.

"Stay on whoever he meets," said Freddy to the surveillance team. "We cannot tip our hand we're on them. So if we don't have four or five tails, we'll use the drone to track with a single trailer hanging back."

"Roger that, ma'am."

Andros turned into the parking lot. There were two other cars. He parked in a space near the end, under a tree. Within minutes, another Harley pulled in. It idled over to him.

The helmeted figure handed him an athletic bag. Even muffled by the lowered visor, he recognized La Sombra's voice.

"Everything you need. Be careful. Check your back. Call me when the delivery is made and the job in El Paso is done."

Andros watched the bike kick gravel as it spun out. That was short and sweet, he thought. Quite the social guy. Won't invite him to my next party.

Tough luck, thought Nick. He never removed his helmet. No chance to ID him. "Freddy, let's stay on the new guy."

"I agree. We know where Andros can be found."

"Follow the new bike. Stay on him," said Freddy to the drone team. She set the tail cars, but with the winding road they wouldn't be able to approach. They'd be depending on the drone. Her monitor followed as it continued up the Alpine Loop. The bike sped through the twists and turns, coming out on East Provo Canyon Road. In Orem, traffic picked up, but the computer controller of the drone stuck to the big Harley. The tail car was a quarter mile back.

"Got him," said Freddy, watching the bike enter a garage of a house. "Agent, not a word of this to anyone." Freddy called off the tail car. The fewer people who knew about this the smaller the chance for a problem. She trusted her people, but…

Now what to do? If she notified Homeland Security, they'd storm the place in a big showy assault. Maybe they'd get him, maybe not. Maybe he'd choose to shoot it out and die. If they did capture him, everything would fall under U. S. laws, and he'd have a lawyer within hours. They had no evidence of any crime. He'd walk.

Making a command decision she'd probably pay for later, Freddy called Nick back.

# Chapter 38

"Nick, whoever Andros met, we have located their house." said Freddy.

"Yeah, I saw. What's your plan?"

She was sure it was Hashim. Should she bring Nick and Katherine in on the capture? They wanted Hashim more than she did. Of course, they'd do the interrogation, but then what? It would be cleaner if they took Hashim from the site right after the capture. She had to trust them, at least for now.

"We're setting up observation cams on his house. I'll bring in everything we can, taps, monitor on cell activity, lasers on the windows for sound pickup. We're going to hang back until we can get him for sure. We'll watch for at least a day to confirm it's Hashim, but I'm ninety percent sure now."

"What do you want us to do?" asked Nick.

"Capture and interrogate him, of course. Just kidding. We'll work together as a team."

"What about your other guys, local LEOs, CIA, and Homeland Security?"

Freddy let out a deep breath. "Bringing them would be the fastest way to fuck this thing up. You and I both know what will happen. It won't be a surprise, he'll flee again. Also, we have nothing solid on him. It would be Katherine's word against his about a kidnapping. We can't use Mohammed's interrogation tapes or those of Joaquin. Any good lawyer would blow up her arrest, make her an unreliable witness. He'd walk."

"Yeah, you're right." Nick knew there were few secrets in government. Everybody tried to gain attention for themselves.

"I'm going to link you into the cams on his house. We'll get floor plans, utilities, and any other information we can. I'll forward it to you as we get it. You and Katherine see what you can come up with. Put a plan together. We'll do the same. In the meantime, I've pulled the units out. We're using the remotes. I'm going to place units in a wide perimeter, so if he leaves, we can follow, and I'll bring in the drone."

"How many know about this so far?" asked Kiki.

"Four, plus me."

"You trust them?"

"Yeah. They're solid with me. Get back with your ideas." This was putting a lot of trust in Nick and Kiki. She mentally crossed her fingers.

With the link to the monitor in the motorhome, Kiki and Nick studied the video of Hashim riding the bike into the garage of the house. It was a wood-frame split-level in a neighborhood with an open field behind. Windows at ground level indicated a basement. How to capture him alive was the problem.

"Could we nail him with tasers when he came out?" asked Kiki. The scene of Hashim standing at the motorhome door shielded by Mohammed came back. She pushed the memory of what followed down. She'd nail him this time, she told herself.

"That would be ideal. Let's use our new resources, get Freddy to check alarm companies to see if there are alarms on the house."

"He might have installed his own," said Kiki.

Nick nodded. "We'll get Freddy to check stores to see if he's bought anything on his own. It's only been a week. He may not have had a chance to alarm the place yet."

"Not knowing what identity he used will make that hard."

"The Feds are good at crunching data. We'll get Freddy to check banks to see who's opened accounts in the last two days. It'll at least give us possible names. They can cross-check for purchases and vehicle buys or leases." Might as well make maximum use of the federal resources, thought Nick.

A troubled expression crossed Kiki's face. "Nick, we can't just smash down the door and barge in. He'll do himself before we can stop him. What about gas? Could we knock him out with that, just go in and get him while he's unconscious?"

Nick grimaced. "That didn't work out too well for the Chechnyan's when the Russians tried it."

"Yeah, but you're talking Russians. There's a difference here. We only have one guy in a house. We can get the plans so we have the exact dimensions." Kiki looked back at the monitor. It was a mission puzzle, something she solved daily in Afghanistan. "Let's call Freddy back. See what she says." Nick reached for the phone.

Nick and Kiki's suggestions had been good. Freddy had her team working on bank accounts and alarm system purchases, trying to cross-check them. Freddy had just closed her office door when the phone rang.

"Freddy, are you alone?" asked Nick.

"I just shooed the last ones out. Yeah. What's up?"

Kiki and Nick told her of their concerns and the gas plan.

"Good thinking on the banks. We're moving on that now. The gas might work if we do it while he's sleeping. Okay, here's what we'll do. When he leaves the next time, we'll take a closer look at the house. If we can bore a small hole in a window frame, say in the basement, we can slowly fill the house.

"I've got guys checking for alarm systems now. If there isn't one, we'll cut the power first. It'll add to confusion if he wakes up. We'll cover all exits with tasers."

"Consider that he might make his own exit through a window or even a wall," said Kiki. "Does he have another vehicle?"

"We think there's a vehicle in the garage, though we haven't seen him drive it. We'll check the banks, then search for any records of him registering one. That doesn't mean anything. He's established at least one new identity we know about. We might miss one. Car dealers take a few days to put the registrations in. He could also buy private or use an alias." It was the best they could do in such a short time.

"Okay, here's the plan," said Kiki. "The next time he leaves, we'll come in over the field behind the house. Let's wear farm clothes, so if we're spotted by the neighbors they'll ignore us. I like the idea of putting a hole in a windowsill. He's not likely to find it, and any noise from the gas won't be noticed."

Freddy's first reaction to Kiki taking charge was to push back. She was in charge. But her plan was good. Let's let her run, Freddy thought. I'd sure like to hire Kiki as a field operative. With Nick, they'd make a great team.

Nick spoke up. "Doing this on the same level as the bedroom will give us better disbursement, as long as doors aren't closed."

"Let's look at the house. He may not keep the door closed. If I were as cautious as he seems, I wouldn't," said Kiki. "I'd want to hear everything. A closed door is a baffle."

Freddy continued. "I like the gas idea; we'll cut the power if no lights are on. We'll push a vehicle into the driveway and block the garage. I count three doors, so we'll cover those, but also the windows."

"If he wakes up, he'll fight, make his own exit," warned Kiki.

"Nick, Katherine," said Freddy, "once we have him, you'll need to secure him and bundle him into your van. Take him wherever you want him. I don't want to know where that is. When you're ready, we'll set up a link so we can follow your interrogation. At that point, I'll bring in Albert Bowman of Homeland Security and Dianne Coleman of CIA. I'm pretty sure we can trust them to let you do your job before seeking glory." She wasn't as sure as that sounded, but there was no choice.

"Yeah, That's the impression I got," said Kiki, nodding. At least from Bowman.

"Okay, Freddy, let us know," said Nick.

Two hours later, alone in her office, Freddy called Nick and Katherine.

"Hashim bought an alarm system this morning. We have to assume he'll install it soon, maybe tomorrow. I think we should consider going in tonight."

Nick looked at Kiki. This was moving fast. Were they ready? "He will install it tonight," said Kiki.

"The system he bought will take a few hours to install. If his lights stay on late, and we hear tools running, we must consider another plan."

Whatever plan B is, wondered Kiki. "Are we going with gas?"

"I have it here in the building. I'm getting gear together to inject it into the spare bedroom through the upstairs window frame. We'll also drill a hole in a downstairs window and put a sensor in. We want to detect when we've filled the house adequately. We're going to follow your plan to come at the back of the house across the field. Let's meet at the Cottonwood Park parking lot as a staging area at 03:00 hours."

"We'll be there," said Kiki.

# Chapter 39

Hashim did a quick check of the house. The tells he left were in place. It was clear. He went to the front window, looking for any sign of a tail or surveillance. He saw none. He returned to the garage and retrieved the packages from the bike. Tomorrow he'd install the alarm system. He also needed to make more thermite and rig the house in case unwelcome visitors showed up.

Thus far, no sign that Mohammed was still alive or had talked. He could not afford to underestimate his enemies. Assumptions that things were okay could get him killed, or worse, captured.

Andros and Charon's Children had done well. The killings in Layton and Las Vegas would not go unnoticed. Hashim smiled to himself. Enemies would be seeking him.

Logging onto his email, he wrote up the status and left it in the Drafts box. The link from Mexico to the Albuquerque Charon's Children would be reestablished, drugs would flow to them. The program would continue. He logged off. Time for bed. He had not recovered from the long trip.

He was asleep as soon as his eyes closed. The same dream returned.

The empty desert of his homeland stretched before him. Hashim's village was at his back as he walked toward the mountains, blue in the distance. He turned for a last look, his wife waved with one hand, holding his son in the other. The explosion shattered his world as the concussion bowled him over.

Stunned, face in the dirt, it came to him. Drone strike! They'd be watching for survivors. He lay still, his tears leaking into the dirt.

He tried to rise, but his arms were so heavy. Let me wake up, he thought. He sank back.


Nick and Kiki were parked behind the black Suburban, peering through the predawn blackness as Freddy and her team unpacked the lightweight aluminum ladder and bag of tools. Two agents strapped pressure tanks to their backs, another picked up a bag of tools. One agent remained behind with the vehicles. Freddy signaled they were ready.

In tight black clothes, the team moved across the open field toward the housing development. No words were spoken. At the line of backyard fences, Freddy consulted her pad. She pointed to the house in front of them, Hashim's house. As they slipped over the fence, a dog three doors away began to bark. They froze, invisible in the shadows. A voice yelled, quieting the dog.

Once in the yard, they moved toward the house. Silently, the ladder was extended to the window Freddy indicated above. One agent climbed upward, a muffled drill in hand. Those below heard nothing as he bored a hole in the wooden windowsill. A hose was passed to him, the other end connected to the pressure tanks. A valve was opened. The agent descended.

The hole boring was repeated at a first-floor window, and a probe was inserted. Now they had to wait.

Nick walked across the field back to the van. He and the remaining agent would move the vehicles to the front of the house upon Freddy's signal.

Thirty minutes later, faces covered with gas masks, the shadowy figures slipped through the back door. In the green light of the night-vision goggles, they quickly moved from room to room, clearing the house. Only Hashim was inside.

Freddy clicked her com unit three times as a signal to move the vehicles to the house. Minutes later, Hashim, gagged and trussed, was carried through the garage to the waiting van.

"Well, that went as planned," said Freddy. "Bit of a surprise, actually." After placing the unconscious Hashim in Nick's van, she dusted her hands. "Call when you're ready for the link." She waved into the darkness as the van pulled away.

Freddy returned to supervise the agents as they went through the house, collecting Hashim's laptop and all evidence they could find. Once gone, there was no sign that Hashim had been there. The holes in the windowsill were patched and painted. They were ghosts.

The highways to Spanish Fork were deserted this early in the morning. The adrenalin buzz was wearing off.

"Nick, do you think Hashim's interrogation will be the same as with Mohammed?" Katherine looked at Nick.

He glanced from the road to her. "He's Muslim. We'll take him to the same place Mohammed was when he told everything to me. We'll take him to Allah."

"I know that, Nick." She looked at him, eyebrows raised. "It's the *other*, I'm talking about."

"I know," responded Nick, an icy tone in his voice. He, too, was nervous about encountering this 'director.' Part of him wanted it to come out, confirm it wasn't in his mind. Another part was fear of this creature.

Freddy's group had collected several things from Hashim's for the computer forensics nerds. It was turning into a good night. Albert Bowers, voice husky with sleep, answered her call.

"Freddy Foster here. We captured Hashim. Meet me at the office. The link-up will be active within two hours to observe the interrogation. You're invited to the party." She felt a little smug, giving him this news, showing him they could operate without help.

"Wha? When did this happen?"

"Just now. We got a hit on the wiretap and moved. There wasn't time to call in anybody else," she lied.

"Where's Hashim now?"

"Sabino and Russell are taking him to their place. We're going to videoconference the interrogation."

"Do we have an agent with them?"

This was a touchy part. Bowers wouldn't be pleased they had turned Hashim over to contractors. "No. That would be a direct link to us. I'm not sure where they are going, but we'll know when the link is set up. We'll meet at the office in an hour." Freddy cut the connection. It was better to answer his questions and concerns face-to-face. Would he chew her ass or congratulate her?

The Spanish Fork RV park was dark when Nick and Kiki arrived. After checking for curious eyes and confirming the motorhome was undisturbed, they carried Hashim in. He regained consciousness, struggled. Kiki knelt on his chest, grabbed his face, and held it forcefully inches away from hers. She enjoyed the shock in his eyes as he recognized her. Hashim's struggles ceased.

Nick bared their captive's arm and injected the anesthetic. Hashim's eyes rolled up. Stripping him, Kiki stared at the scars, scars of war and torture. These were on the outside. What about the ones inside this man, she wondered.

Once Nick had him plugged in, they placed Hashim in the isolation chamber. With feelings of apprehension, they closed the lid. Was 'the other, the director' inside Hashim? Would their questioning bring it out? Was it real? Nick shoved those doubts aside.

Watching the pulse rate, breathing rate and brainwave activity, Nick added the stimulants to wake him. The curarine level paralyzed him.

Monitors spiked as he regained consciousness. Hashim screamed. They let him continue. His heart raced as he struggled to move. At last, the cries became Arabic words.

"Where am I? Where is the devil Katherine Russell? Has she killed me?"

Nick looked at Kiki. She stared daggers at the isolation chamber. Nick remembered the director telling him how he'd pushed the hatred level up in Kiki with Ramón. He remembered the look of evil that crossed her face. Was the director doing it again? He'd have to watch her. With a deep breath, Nick started.

*"Hashim, you are no longer in your old world. You are with me now. You must prepare to enter Paradise, you must make a song of your life so that all will know you."*

There was no voice, but the words were in his brain. His skull vibrated with them. "Allah, where am I?"

*"You are at the gates of Paradise. Begin your song with yesterday. Sing of your exploits, your triumphs, your challenges. Sing a song of your service to me."*

Nick and Kiki sat in the small bedroom of the motorhome as Hashim's song filled the air. Nick understood the Arabic, translating for Kiki. The FBI translator in the conference room occasionally asked him for a clarification. It went on for hours.

Nick pushed back from the laptop. The red light of the link camera wavered before his eyes, the traces of the monitors showing Hashim's vital signs blurred. He shook his head to clear it. Kiki put a hand on his shoulder to steady him.

"I need a rest. He needs a rest. I'm putting him to sleep until tomorrow. We can't afford a mistake. We'll call you at noon to set up the link and continue," Nick said in a weary voice.

"Yeah, we're tired, too," said Agent Bowman. "Thanks, Nick. Great job."

Nick shut down the link and rubbed his eyes.

**"Hello, Nick. Are you waiting for me? Of course you are. Hello, Katherine. My, my, even though Nick told you of me, you are surprised."**

Kiki froze, staring at the speakers. Nick saw the shock on her face as she turned toward him, mouth open.

**"Nick, there is relief in you that I am real. I told you so. Katherine was a little worried about you, too. So, Katherine, you have been waiting for me, have you not?"**

Kiki asked, "You're in Hashim?"

*"Among others. Right, Nick? I am in many. I am in those who are questioning Mohammed right now. They have some delicious hatred, and Mohammed's fear is wonderfully tangy. Their frustration at getting nothing from him swells that hatred. It is really quite tasty. I do not think Mohammed will survive much longer."*

"What do you want? Why are you here? What are you?"

*"Katherine, I know Nick told you about me. You did not understand because you thought Nick was losing sanity. He is not. I am of a race of spirits dwelling within you. I feed on your emotions. My particular tastes favor hatred and fear. I place suggestions and images in your mind to enhance those emotions. You are my food."*

"Your food!" screamed Kiki. Her hands flew to her head as laughter echoed.

Nick went to her. He felt her shake as his hands rested on her shoulders. "K, it's not physical. It can't do anything to you."

**"How touching. Nick is right though. Physically I can do nothing to you. Mentally is another thing. Katherine, before you returned to the United States, you controlled your hatred so well. It has gotten out of hand lately, has it not?"**

Kiki's mind recoiled at the truth of this.

**"I do have to thank you. During your tours in Afghanistan, you were one of my best tools. The fear and hatred you induced in your enemies made for many a delicious meal for me."**

"Nick, turn it off," she screamed, pointing at the speaker.

He flipped the switch to kill the sound system.

**"Did Nick forget to tell you that would not work? I am inside you."**

The words echoed in her head. Kiki shuddered. Inside her! She explored her own mind, opening one door after another. Get out! Get out of my head. She looked wildly around the room. Her eyes came to rest on the isolation chamber.

**"Ah, and now you hate and fear me. That is a new combination of flavors from you."**

Nick saw a look of panic on Kiki's face. He knew what was happening. He pulled her into his arms. "Kiki, think of me, think of your husband, think of your parents. You have to take away its food so it will leave you alone. It feeds on your hatred and fear."

Kiki struggled to find a thought. Her mind flew through her memories, seeking something she could settle on. Her mother! They were riding together in Pinetop. She was on her horse, Nichol. She patted the horse's neck as birds tweeted and flitted through the sunbeam streaks filtering through the trees. Nichol had been her closest friend since she was ten. He nickered softly at her touch. The clear sky was the deep blue only seen at high altitude. The fragrance of pines filled her, and the silence of the trail was overpowering. Peace settled upon her.

# Chapter 40

Freddy was getting pressure to obtain results against the dependent murder program. Her boss had been questioned in a press conference about whether an unusually high murder rate was taking place against military dependents. He'd sidestepped the issue, saying he would check.

Freddy got the job of bringing him up to speed. She struggled over the prepared statement for her boss. It had to sound like they were aware of an anomaly in the rate of attacks and looking into it. They did not want to reveal that this was a terrorist attack on American soil. They did not want to alert their enemies to the extent of what they knew or that they had captives. We need time.

The knock on her door startled her. Dianne Coleman smiling. Freddy closed her laptop, pushing it to the side of the desk in her temporary office in Salt Lake City.

"Dianne, how's your questioning of Mohammed going?" Mohammed was with Dianne's CIA team, who had more experience in interrogating Arab suspects.

"We got nothing. As soon as he woke up, he started screaming. That hasn't stopped. We've sedated him again to save his throat. We're feeding and hydrating him with IVs. Honestly, I don't think he's going to come out of this." Coleman shook her head. "He's a total zero."

"After what Nick told us, I'm not surprised," replied Freddy. "I tried to imagine what would happen to me if I was brought back from the gates of heaven only to find I'd betrayed everything I believed."

Coleman's lips tightened. "That's why this type of interrogation is outlawed by United Nation agreement. Waterboarding was borderline. We got good information. We had to check everything from different directions to confirm it, like sifting through sand looking for the nuggets. It was slow and tedious work, taking weeks, sometime months to break them down."

"If you believe the end justifies the means, we need Nick and Katherine," said Freddy staring at the desk. "I'm not going to lie and say we'll only allow it for this crisis. There's always another crisis. That's the trap."

"We're talking aboutsaving American lives, innocent lives here!" exclaimed Dianne.

"That's the quandary we face. Do we give up our souls for security? Do we become those we abhor? Doesn't the value of human life apply to us?" Freddy shook her head. She looked at Dianne, seeking understanding. It wasn't there.

"I was impressed with the quality of information Nick and Katherine got from Hashim," said Dianne. She flicked her hair from her eyes, leaned forward toward Freddy. "Their techniques are sophisticated and exact. They didn't reveal exactly how they did it, but Nick has a talent for keeping the captive's mind on the edge of reality." A thin-lipped smile crossed her face. "Nick is able to lead him through his life so he willingly gives us what we need. He accomplishes in hours what took us weeks. And his accuracy to date has been bang on."

Freddy watched her cross her arms, a smug look on her face as she said, "With the information he got from Mohammed, we'll get a team in Mexico to shut down the pipeline of drugs. It also gives us an inroad into the outlaw motorcycle gangs."

Astounded by the idea, Freddy asked, "You're going to put an American team into Mexico?"

Dianne chuckled. "We don't need to do that. We'll contract with a team of Israelis already there. The Mexican government hired them a few years ago to fight the cartels. None of their own people could be trusted. The Israelis have proven very successful. It would be useful to have Nick and Katherine interrogate for us in conjunction with the Israelis."

Freddy wasn't happy. "I'm not sure we should send them to Mexico. There's an added risk of establishing a secure base, and we certainly don't want to lose them. Are you thinking of using them for more than this program?"

Dianne smiled. "The Mexicans will pay us well for quality information. We will be helping a friendly government and ourselves."

Freddy was dismayed by Dianne's attitude. She seemed careless of Kiki and Nick's safety. "Dianne, the problem is that the threat to Nick and Katherine grows exponentially as more people know about them. In Mexico, we really don't have control. It would only be a matter of time before we lose them." She realized that everybody was a tool to Dianne, even her.

"You're right. What if we put them in Guantanamo?"

"I'm afraid that with relations normalizing in Cuba, we won't have that base much longer. And the problem with Nick and Katherine's interrogations is the aftermath. What do we do with the prisoners? What are you going to do with Mohammed? What are we going to do with Hashim?"

"That question has come up. For Mohammed, it may be a quiet burial in Potter's Field. I have no doubt that when we get Hashim, he'll be in the same condition. Meet the same end." She held up her hands and shrugged. An idea occurred to Dianne. "Maybe we could use a Navy ship for interrogations. We'd certainly have better control."

This was getting worse. Freddy shook her head. "Would the Navy go along? You'd have to inform more people. The Joint Chiefs would have to be informed. Where would it go from there? As of right now, the President maintains deniability. Only a few others know the real story. Any effort to expand this and the exposure goes up for everyone, including us. If the shit hits the fan, we'll be the ones looking like pinto ponies. Keep that in mind." CIA spooks had a different political mindset, Freddy realized. They were used to working in the dark.

Dianne held up her hands, palms toward Freddy. "Okay, let's table that for now. Unfortunately, Mohammed and Hashim didn't give us enough to wipe out the Mexican side or the OMGs in the U. S. That ,is why I wanted to work that end. We could use them to work the Middle Eastern side too, but it has the same problem. The last thing we need is another Abu Ghraib. Our eyes are still black from that."

# Chapter 41

Nick and Kiki glanced at the camera transmitting the interrogation of Hashim. The alphabet soup federal government group had been observing live feed of Hashim's interrogations. This would be his last session. He had little information to add to the American operations. CIA Agent Dianne Coleman wanted to know more about the Afghanistan operations and of Hashim's early life.

Nick glanced at the dull black isolation chamber. It had been their tool for tracking these bastards down, but now he sensed an aura like a foul odor surrounding it. He checked the vital sign monitors, adjusted the drips and watched as the traces showed Hashim waking.

"Allah, am I ready to enter Paradise?"

*"Hashim, your song is not complete. Tell the story of your life in Afghanistan, your life following my teaching,"* Nick said into the microphone.

"My village was small and poor…" Hashim began.

Nick, Kiki, and the investigation team listened to the birth and making of a jihadist.

Hashim told of the death of those in his village by drone attack, invasion and torture by Afghan government forces. He recounted his boyhood recruitment into the extremist sect. He trained in Nigeria and Libya, returning to active battle. His talent at languages singled him out for training as a recruiter in foreign lands before he was sent to America for this program. His brother was martyred by the Iblis sniper, Katherine Russell.

When he finished, Nick adjusted the drips. Kiki watched the government team on the monitor, studying every move Nick made. She had no doubt Dianne Coleman would study the tapes intently. The vital signs drifted down, showing Hashim going to sleep.

"We've milked Hashim dry," said Kiki to the monitor. "We'll bring him to you at the Salt Lake office. The sooner the better."

Dianne Coleman's image filled the screen. "Katherine, Nick, the information Hashim has given us is invaluable, but it would be so much more useful if you would help us in Afghanistan. We now have targets to go after. We want to send you there after we finish with the terrorist program here and the connections in Mexico."

"You want to keep using us?" asked Nick. "I thought there'd be an end, that we'd go back to normal lives."

"Oh, you will," said Dianne, "just as soon as we finish. We need your help with the Mexican connection. We'll be paying you well for your service. You can go back to civilian lives knowing you helped defeat these enemies."

Kiki and Nick looked at each other. Oh sure, they mouthed simultaneously.

"We'll talk this over," stalled Kiki, "and get back to you."

"Katherine," said Coleman, "we are going to pick up Andros. We want you to interrogate him. His people killed the family in Logan and the other family in Las Vegas. We need your help to shut down the Charon's Children gang before they kill more families."

Nick didn't like the tone of this. Freddy was supposed to be their boss, but Dianne sounded like she was in charge. "Let us know when you have him. We'll arrange an exchange for Hashim."

"We will."

They broke the connection. Kiki gave Nick a hard look. They both had seen the shift of power.

"Nick, who's going to direct Charon's Children, now that we have Hashim? We've broken the chain in America. The feds want to go after Charon's Children for drugs and racketeering, using us to do it."

"K, these guys did the actual killing, but I think it's the same in Mexico. Our role is moving beyond the terrorist program in America." This was rapidly spinning out of their control. They held no high cards in the game.

"Nick, knowing about this Presence, this *mental virus*, has changed me. Since it feeds on my hatred, I'm guarded about letting it out."

"I know, K. I don't hold that hatred like I used to. Part of that is because I don't want to feed the director, but I now have more understanding of our enemies. The job to protect our people hasn't changed, but the drive to do it is no longer fueled by hatred. Hashim told us of what shaped him into the fighter he is now. If I'd been through his life, I'm not sure how different I'd be. The West is not blameless in this."

Kiki's dark brown eyes shifted from the isolation chamber to Nick. "When I found out about my family, the hatred for those responsible was so intense it took over my being. They did it for drugs and money, not for a cause or belief. I still hate them. I have no regrets for wiping them out. The world is better off with them gone," she said with finality. "Now, I'm a lot more guarded in my hatred. The idea of feeding that thing. Ugh!" she winced.

Nick nodded. It was better without them, but…"K, when we were interrogating them, I saw the forces that formed their lives. To say that they chose is not entirely correct. They certainly reached points when they chose evil, but what set them up for that? If they had known they were being manipulated by the director, would it have made a difference?"

Nick paused, shaking his head before continuing. "Director! Hah! It's not going to direct me anymore. It is the awareness of this Presence that has changed me. I can see the influence."

"It's the same for me. The passion for this job is fading." She tried to look ahead, wondering what will I do? she thought. It's not like I have a marketable skill set.

# Chapter 42

Through the rain, Nick backed the van into the delivery ramp next to the ambulance at the Salt Lake City federal building. Two people dressed in hospital scrubs stepped from the roll-up doorway. Freddy opened the back door of the ambulance as Nick and Kiki got out.

"How did you capture him?" Nick nodded to the covered figure.

Freddy glanced at the stretcher. "It wasn't too hard. Andros is arrogant, never making a secret of his movements, unless he is directly involved in something. He's a creature of habit. This morning, we waited at his house for him to arrive. Tased him as he got off his bike."

"Anybody with him?" asked Kiki.

"Usually, Andros wants to be around people, showing off his superiority I don't think he likes his own company. He had one of his guys with him, who chose to fight it out. Didn't make it. Andros is unhurt, except for the anesthetic."

"What about Hashim?" asked Dianne Coleman.

Nick opened the side door of the van.

"Is he in the same shape as Mohammed?" Coleman asked.

Kiki gave her a sharp look. "This interrogation is a one-way street. You don't come back from it. You can try to bring him back," she nodded at the unconscious figure, " but I believe those chances are slim. Just like Mohammed, there's not a person in there anymore."

Dianne motioned to two men emerging from the doorway. They lifted Hashim by the arms and dragged him into the ambulance, Andros into the van.

"We need your help with the Mexican end and then Afghanistan," said Dianne.

"Nick and I are burning out. I'm not sure that's a good idea."

"We're going to need your help on the Mexican end and then Afghanistan," repeated Dianne, giving Kiki a cold stare.

Kiki pressed her lips together and walked away. Wordlessly, she and Nick got in the van and drove into the storm.

Freddy and Dianne watched them go. "They'll do it," said Dianne, a smug expression on her face. She watched Freddy shake her head. "They have no choice."

Unlike the two Arabs, Andros was a big man. With Kiki and Nick under each arm, they struggled to get him up the steps and into the motorhome. Nick kept a Taser ready in case the feds had misjudged the dosage keeping him unconscious. He could do serious damage if he started thrashing around.

As they undressed him, his battle wounds were apparent and numerous. So was the ink. Tattoos covered the upper torso, some looking like gulag tats. There was no religious ink.

Kiki and Nick looked at the isolation chamber then each other.

Nick looked at the floor. "K, I have a bad feeling about this contract. I'm not sure we can turn down a job or walk away." He looked up to see her eyes locked onto him.

"Me, either." She felt cold fear and quickly suppressed it. Don't give the Presence anything, she said to herself. "We either continue to deal with these people or disappear." Her lips were a tight line.

In a soft voice, Nick said, "K, we may not disappear by our choice. I've been keeping records for insurance, but it may not be enough."

Kiki heard chuckling in her mind. Oh, no, she thought. Not now.

The whispery voice echoed within her. ***"This is a delicious taste from you. You are afraid of yourself if you do not quit. Fear of yourself is particularly bitter. I like it."***

Kiki had always considered her personal insight a helpful talent. Now she cursed it. Eyes closed, fists clenched, she screamed, "Get out! I cannot deal with you and this situation at the same time."

***"I will leave you alone for now, but I am here. Ta ta for now."***

Nick came over and put his arm around her. The tone for the communication system from the feds started beeping. They ignored it. Grunting and heaving, they got Andros into the chamber and connected to the monitors and IV. As they closed the chamber, Kiki realized with a tremor that they were sending another body into the void.

Nick checked the monitors and the IV drips, adjusting them as necessary to keep Andros immobilized. When he began bringing Andros back to consciousness, Kiki looked at Nick. Her face asked if they were ready for this. She called the feds.

"Why didn't you answer when I called," snapped Dianne.

"We were a little busy. Andros isn't a small guy," Kiki retorted.

"Are you ready to start the interrogation?" asked Freddy, her voice trying to keep the tone on a professional level.

"We're bringing him up now," Nick said.

"We need more light," said Dianne. "It's hard to see what you're doing."

Kiki turned with a sharp retort but Nick held out his hand to calm her. Antagonizing Coleman would not gain them anything. Kiki turned on a small lamp, changing the room from dark to dim. The isolation chamber seemed to suck this light from this room. In the silence, Nick watched Andros' vital signs increase as he awakened. He had no inkling if Andros was religious. None of his tats showed that. He wore no religious symbols. If he were not a believer, how was Nick going to get him to open up? As awareness returned, he would wonder if he were dead or alive. His senses would tell him nothing. He would be a consciousness floating in a void. If he weren't dead, where was he? Why couldn't he feel his body?

Andros would wonder why was he here? Where was here? This wouldn't be the endless sleep he imagined.

Nick hummed softly into the microphone. He watched Andros' pulse and breathing increase as he heard the sound in his head.

"What is that? Is someone there?" shouted Andros. His ears heard no sound, not even his own shouts. Did he shout? Of course he did. "I know that's not God. There is no God!" he yelled. He heard nothing. Andros hated being by himself. How long would this last? The reality of eternity with nothing dawned on him. Nick watched Andros' pulse rate, breathing, and brainwave activity accelerate rapidly. The heart trace showed a few skipped beats. It was something he'd have to watch. Nick decided on a strategy for Andros.

"Freddy, Dianne, we're going to let him alone for a while. No questions for a few hours," said Nick.

"Wait a minute," snarled Dianne. "You're not getting out of this."

"Andros is an atheist, at least for now. Let's see what happens when he has only himself in his universe. I'll call you when we begin to question him." Nick left no doubt who was running this. He nodded at Kiki.

She closed the link with a satisfying push of the button. She hated this, being forced to do things. "I'm learning to despise that woman. Coleman's attitude doesn't help soften the blow of being a slave."

**"Oh, this is delicious! Nick, Katherine, you never cease to deliver. Your efforts to temper your fear is a tasty appetizer. Perhaps I can push Andros harder. Thank you."**

Kiki and Nick looked at each other, eyes wide. That's when the screaming started.

# Chapter 43

As an atheist, Andros didn't prove as difficult to question as they feared. After one hour, Nick added sedative. Andros' screaming began to subside. Nick hummed into the microphone again.

"Who is that?" asked Andros.

*"It's me, you idiot. There's nobody else here but me,"* Nick growled.

"You're me?"

*"Who else would I be?"*

"So those assholes shot me? I'm dead?"

*"See anything? Feel anything? I don't think so,"*

"This is all there is? There's no one else?"

*"Were you hoping for God? You were hoping for streets paved with gold, winged creatures soaring overhead?"*

"Nah, I never believed in that shit. But I thought I'd end up in hell, if there was one. I done some bad shit."

*"Yeah, like killing that family in Layton. Cutting off their heads. That was pretty nasty."*

"That wasn't my idea. La Sombra wanted that."

*"So why did you do what he wanted?"*

"He paid in pure heroin. Good money."

*"Yeah, but you probably got killed because of him. You knew those killings and beheadings would bring in the big dogs."*

"Yeah, guess I did. Thought I could handle them. So how long do I stay here?"

*"Forever, you idiot! And yeah, you only have yourself to talk to. You can't just float around. Might as well talk about it all – the things you regret, the things you liked, the things you hated – got nothing else to do but review your life and remember."*

"What do I do after that?"

*"Do it again…and again."*

Nick wasn't giving Andros any room. He would pile eternity alone on his head until he broke. He clamped down on rising hatred. He didn't need the Presence.

"K, can you bring me some water? This is going to be a long session."

"Nick, let's take it in shifts. I can say the stuff needed to keep him going."

"Thanks, K."

"Freddy, we're not getting anything to help with the terrorist investigation from Andros," said Nick. "He doesn't know anything."

She answered. "But we're getting information on Outlaw Motorcycle Gangs. Andros knows a lot about drug distribution and suppliers, especially meth. It's good information. It'll help us shut down some big organized crime operations. These guys deal in drugs, gambling, prostitution, contract killings, theft, robberies, and extortion operations. They are bad people."

"So you're using us now on crime investigations?" asked Kiki.

"That wasn't our intent," Coleman broke in. "We need to pursue the terrorist connection in Mexico. This leads back to radical Islam. That's our enemy."

"Nick and I haven't decided whether we want to continue beyond the U. S. borders," said Kiki.

"Does that mean you're going to quit, or just wait for the next attacks within the borders?" asked Dianne, snidely.

Kiki closed the connection.

"Nick, what are we going to do?" Kiki looked at him, eyes pleading for an answer.

He smiled humorlessly "I knew this was a deal with the devil when I made it, but I had to get you back."

"Thank you for that. Things didn't get ugly at Guantanamo, but they easily could have. I now feel differently toward those prisoners. I also feel differently toward the word terrorism. It seems to apply to anyone who opposes the U. S. efforts, yet the things we do are just as bad."

Nick shook his head. Once upon a time, he would have rejected that idea vehemently. "We don't use people as tools. We don't commit uncivilized acts against them to elicit a reaction. We don't do that." Even as he said it, he knew it wasn't true.

"That said, K, I'm feeling differently toward our enemies, too. Our interrogations are a death sentence for them, if not in body, certainly in mind. When we expose their souls, it's not hard to understand what made them who they are. What would I have done under similar circumstances?"

"Nick, I understand that we have to protect our people and our soldiers, but the hatred isn't there anymore."

*"If I were not so fond of you both, I would go elsewhere. The compassion you are showing is a sweet and sour flavor not to my liking. Your world is full of the emotions I like. You still bring me great tastes in others. Our conversations are much more interesting than those with my other selves. This is fun."*

"So sorry to disappoint you," snapped Kiki. "Maybe you should go somewhere else."

*"No reason to get snippy. It is just an observation. You have become more like the leaders. They do not hate nearly as much as those carrying out their orders. That is where my tasty treats lie."*

"I'm taking that as a compliment," said Kiki.

*"Perhaps it is to you. Leaders have little to fear. I do like to tweak them. That is especially easy with religious leaders who need intolerance and hatred to bolster their position. They spur their followers to*

*perform nasty acts against their fellow men, which generates great hatred and fear, a feast for me. Leaders do this in the name of God and love. Is that not ironic?"*

"You make leaders sound emotionless," said Nick.

*"Oh no. They have greed, whether it is for power or material goods. Greed is sharply bitter, not to my taste. Envy is too sour. Greed and envy are like appetizers."*

"I didn't realize there was so much difference," said Nick, a hard tone in his voice.

*"You both are unique because you are now aware of us. It has changed you, not to my advantage. But I still like you."*

"We both were raised to believe in good and evil, God and the Devil," said Nick.

*"Good and evil are subjective terms you apply. We simply are. You are here to feed us. We do not care how you define us, because we do not know good or evil."*

"You keep saying 'us.' You're saying there are more of you?" asked Kiki.

*"I told you, there are more of us."*

"You don't care that you are responsible for millions of deaths?" cried Kiki.

*"They are all going to die eventually. Just as you add spices and herbs to flavor your food, I do the same. Does your pot roast care about salt? Moreover, do you care if it matters to your pot roast? You flavor to your taste. I do the same."*

"But we're thinking and caring beings!" exclaimed Nick.

*"That is a matter of opinion."*

Kiki put her hands to her head. "Nick, I have to get away from this!"

*"Get away? Nick told you I am part of you. You cannot get away. I will leave you alone for a while. There is a great feast in North Africa I am going to. After that, another in Iraq. Ta ta."*

Kiki looked at Nick, silently pleading for a way out of this nightmare. "Nick, what are we going to do?"

He creased his brow. "I don't know. I think of it as a mental virus."

"A mental virus? Can we make an antivirus?"

Nick's shoulders sagged. "I don't know what that would be. This is not a physical virus, so an antivirus would not be a physical thing. First things first, K.

"We have to figure out what to do with this contract with the feds. When we were fighting terrorists, it seemed right. After exploring the minds of these men, knowing this mental virus is at the heart of the hatred and violence, I feel we are fighting the wrong enemy."

"I feel the same, Nick. What are we going to do about it?" Her eyes were pleading for an answer. "What can we do about it?"

"We have to plan carefully, K, very carefully."

# Chapter 44

"Damn them! We're losing them," shouted Dianne Coleman, slamming her hand on the table.

"Why do you think Nick and Katherine are resisting further work for us?" asked Freddy. As if she didn't know. Nick and Kiki were first rate, but they resisted being pushed where they didn't want to go. They had to be led, not pushed.

"I'm not sure. They both have reason enough to keep going after terrorists. They both fought them in Afghanistan. Katherine has personal reasons for hating them," answered the CIA agent. "Nick is there mostly for Katherine."

Freddy nodded. "What's changed?"

"We've seen this from some of our interrogators in the past. They begin to identify with their targets on some level." Dianne shrugged. "Once that starts, we pull them out of the field because their effectiveness wanes." She shook her head.

"Can we reengage them?" Freddy wondered aloud. These interrogations and operations were the territory of the CIA, not the FBI. Power was shifting, and she wasn't comfortable with it.

"Possibly, but it could involve risks. Before trying that, let's put pressure on them to stay. We need them to train another team. I'll begin a search for new candidates."

"Who do we go after next? The Mexican connection?"

Dianne nodded. "That's what I think. We want to get as much from Nick and Katherine as possible. We need to shut down the Western Hemisphere operations, starting with Mexico. It represents the most direct threat to us. We can persuade them to help us with that."

Freddy stared hard at Dianne. "If we're going beyond U. S. borders, Homeland Security will be out. The FBI can only remain involved with your request."

"I'll submit a request tomorrow. It won't be a problem."

"As much as I hate to give up the intelligence about organized crime, we must use them only for terrorist activity," said Freddy.

Typical military, thought Dianne, able to compartmentalize. Anything other than their moral directive, and they sidestep. Can't see the bigger picture. "I'll begin a search for a site to set up. We'll kidnap our targets, something not easily done. Cartel leaders are well guarded. I do have an idea," Dianne smiled. "It's a team we've used before, but we may have to share information."

"Let's put together a plan and conference with Nick and Katherine in a few days." Freddy stood. Something about this woman wasn't right. I've got to be careful not to get sucked into her agenda.

"By then I'll have more info on our alternatives," confirmed Dianne.

Nick tidied up in mindless action. Thoughts and scenarios were swirling in his head. "K, we're going to have to keep helping with the anti-terror campaign."

"I know, Nick. It is a duty, but…"

"K, my hatred of these people is gone, but my determination to protect our citizens is not. I'm going to try something to see how far they will go to keep us working."

Kiki looked at the floor, then up at Nick. Carefully, she let some of her emotion out. "I still hate the terrorists for what they did to my family, but I don't want to feed the virus. A nudge from it, and I could let that consume me. It likes my fear of that. I feel trapped, like a treed animal. What's left?"

"I'm here for you, K. I always will be."

*"Oh, boo hoo."*
The voice filled their heads

*"If you two keep expressing love, another of us will move in. It likes sweet flavors. It may not be as sociable as I."*
"Will it talk to us like you do?" asked Kiki.

*"Maybe, but only if you listen. Of course, it will not possess my witty discourse. Some of us like the bitter flavor of guilt, others like the salty flavor of sorrow. Joy and love are both sweet though joy is more intense but fleeting. As I told you, I like the spicy flavor of hate and the sour taste of fear. The whole crowd might be here, everybody trying to direct you. It could get confusing. I am just saying."*
"What if we don't listen?" asked Kiki. The visions of multiple voices in her head causing her hands to go to her head.

*"That would be disappointing for me. I enjoy talking with you. When you are listening to me, you at least know what to expect. Others are cunning when they try to direct you. You may not be able to recognize the directions."*

"We want the one of love," said Kiki. She looked at Nick, who nodded.

*"Oh bah! That one is so namby-pamby. Choosing greatly depends on you. Picking only one would eliminate those wanting guilt and sorrow in addition to me. But your preference is based on the line you have been sold that love is better than hate. In reality, it does not matter. They are just emotions."*

"But our churches teach rewards for good behavior and punishment for bad behavior," said Nick.

*"Ah, yes, religion. After all, who defines good or evil? Imagine if it were all a lie. What if there were no afterlife for*

*you? What if you had no soul? What if this life is all there is?"*

"I don't believe that!" shouted Kiki. "There has to be more." This was so foreign to everything she'd been taught, she recoiled, trying to push any credibility of this idea away.

*"If that is what you choose to believe. But those of us favoring love and joy are no different from me or the rest. They just like different tastes. They do direct religion as a way of flavoring their food. Some of us get great fun interfering with those directions and corrupting the religious message. It is easy to hate on religious grounds. It creates an interesting flavor, a blend of sweet and spicy. I actually enjoy it."*

"So what you're saying is we should act however we feel is right?"

*"Humans do that anyway. It is the definition of right that varies. What you may find interesting is that your leaders normally taste quite different. They act to*

*inflame their followers. Yet few have the passionate emotions within themselves that they use to control their supporters. They live to direct, much as we do. They feed off the power they wield to control others. I find that thirst for power a rich flavor, like a dessert. I savor it after a great feed. It is an easy emotion to direct because I have only to tickle their ego a bit."*

"Is there no Supreme Being, one who cares for us?" wailed Kiki.

*"I guess if you considered all of us together, we could be defined as such. But we only care for you as a rancher cares for his herd."*

Kiki looked at Nick. He asked the question in both of their minds.

"What happens to us after we die?" asked Nick. He knew what the answer would be, but dreaded hearing it. How could he believe this thing?

**_"You are dead."_**

"I will not let you steal Heaven and my God from me!" cried Kiki. This thing could not destroy the very basis of their belief. Without good and bad, chaos would reign. She felt as if the floor were dropping away.

**_"Perhaps your belief is right, for you. By our observation, it is not."_**

# Chapter 45

Nick and Kiki sat in a small café having a late breakfast. Last night with Andros had been tedious. His memories began to change after numerous repetitions. Freddy found useful information but Dianne had little interest in domestic criminal activity.

"We need to get rid of Andros," said Nick. "His mind is weakening. I don't want a body to take care of."

"We'll insist they take him," said Kiki.

Nick called Freddy.

"Nick, I was about to call you."

"You need to take Andros back. He's weakening, and we have nowhere to keep him. When he's conscious, he screams."

"We need to conference. Can you get back to your base and link up?"

"Yeah, we'll be back in thirty minutes. We'll call you from there."

The tone signaling a linkup sounded. In the monitor, they saw only Dianne Coleman and Freddy Foster in the view of Freddy's office.

"Nick, Katherine, bring Andros by tonight. We'll take him," said Freddy.

"We can be there at seven-thirty," said Kiki.

"We must go after the Mexican connection to the terrorists. We need your help," said Dianne. "I understand your reluctance to travel outside of the United States, but there are complications bringing terrorists here."

"What if I told you we want out?" said Nick. "What if we refuse to continue?"

"You two committed serious crimes for which you could be locked up. We could hold you without trial as witnesses in terrorist acts against the United States. Are you sure you want that?" asked Dianne.

"I see that our "out" clause in the contract is worthless. You do realize who you're threatening," said Kiki, cold hardness in her voice.

They glared at each other in silence.

"Okay, let's calm down," said Freddy. "Nobody's threatening anybody here. We need your help. You understand how important it is we shut down the assassination program, and the Mexican connection is critical. What if we brought the suspects to you? Would you be comfortable doing the interrogations on a boat?"

Nick and Kiki looked at each other. She shook her head no.

"We'd consider that," said Nick.

Kiki's jaw dropped.

"Let us make arrangements and get back to you. As to Andros, bring him to the headquarters service ramp tonight. Call when you leave your place."

"We'll be there at seven-thirty," repeated Kiki. She broke the connection.

She turned to Nick, hands on her hips. "A boat! That will involve a team to capture, another group to transport, and the boat crew. That's a lot of people to watch. And we have no way to run."

Nick held up a hand to ward off her objections. "Those are also my feelings. With Coleman's comment regarding prosecution, we know our contract is rubbish. It is impossible to run and hide on a boat. We'd be at their mercy."

"Then why did you go along with the boat idea?" stormed Kiki.

"We have to play along while we plan an escape from this mess. Running isn't enough." Nick grimaced. "We'd be doing that the rest of our lives. I'm going to call Ramón, our Cayman contact overseeing our bank deposits, and get us new identities, just in case. I believe the boat they're talking about will be in the Caribbean. Maybe we should consider a boat too. I'll have Ramón look into that while he's getting the IDs together."

Freddy looked at Dianne. "That comment about prosecution wasn't good. You did threaten them. I for one don't want to threaten these people. The thought of having them after me scares me shitless."

"We can handle them. They're just two people. I like the idea of the boat," said Dianne. "You thinking of Navy or Coastguard?"

"Neither. We have yachts we've confiscated in drug interdictions. We'll use one of those. It's a smaller crew. What do you have in mind for the capture team in Mexico?"

"We'll contract one of the Israeli hit teams in place to fight cartels. They already have most of the information on the gang we need, so it won't take much time to be up and running."

"Israeli! The Mexican government has contracted with the Israelis?"

"More than the government. Some of the contracts are from a coalition of businesses rather than the government. It's what's kept Cancún open. It was the only way for them to keep corruption out of the anti-cartel war. That has to stay very quiet. Any word and the cartels would attack the businesses.”

“What are we going to do with Andros?” asked Freddy.

“Like Mohammed and Hashim, he’s milked dry of information. We won’t get any more from him. None of them have an anchor in reality. We’re going to warehouse them in a facility for the insane.”

“It’s what they deserve,” said Freddy.

# Chapter 46

*"I must consider you as caterers. Your control of your hatred and fear has moved you off my menu, but I truly do enjoy conversing with you. Talking to my others has gotten so boring."*

With Andros hanging unconscious half out of the isolation chamber, Nick and Kiki froze.

*"You have given me some delicious flavors in Dianne and Freddy. They fear you, yet hate that you are invaluable to their careers. It is a tasty mix. Dianne is particularly jealous of your talent and success. The Islamists are also starting to worry. Their operatives have disappeared with no word. They do not know who they are fighting nor what this foe knows. You have really spiced things up for me."*

They looked at each other and walked from the motorhome and away from any listening devices. "I'm so glad we could accommodate you," sneered Kiki. She felt like spitting on the ground. "If you can read my mind, you can see the loathing I feel for you."

*"I cannot read minds, only sense emotions and deduce thoughts from that. Your hatred for me is also a new taste. I have never dealt with anyone who recognized me before. There is a sourness that is not pleasant to me."*

"How terrible for you. Should I say a prayer?" mocked Kiki.

*"In religion, I have been labeled the devil and hated for that, but it is a shortsighted view. Their hatred is not nearly as intense as yours. It lacks understanding. They hate an ideal. Since you know me, I might suggest some things to you."*

"Suggest! Why not direct, like you do with everyone else?" asked Nick.

*"You would recognize the directions and might reject them because of that, regardless of the value. My suggestion is that you proceed with your plan to escape. Dianne Coleman's greed for power means she must keep you both, even if that means holding one hostage to keep the other in line. She feels powerful enough to go ahead and try. She has shown satisfaction in being in control; she never submitted your contract. That would mean the signatures are forged. She must be paying you out of discretionary funds for informants to keep this hidden from her superiors."*

Nick and Kiki gasped. Betrayed!

*"I detect nothing in Freddy Foster to indicate she knows or participates in this. Freddy takes pride in abiding by the terms of the agreement. She does not agree with Dianne, but she harbors some fear and will not oppose her."*

Nick looked at Kiki. "Why are you helping us?" he asked.

*"As I told you, I like you. You are the first to have an understanding. It allows me to communicate with you. And your knowledge of me brings on new flavors."*

"Tell us more about you and the others," said Kiki. If they were going to fight this thing, they needed to know more.

*"Perhaps a good analogy would be that you are like fish in the sea, we are like birds in the air. Our worlds are completely different, but occasionally we interact. As I told you before, we feed on your emotions. Our only interest in you is to elicit tasty meals. For us, there is no good or evil. We*

*are on another plane without time or space. We do not care for you, only what you can give us. You are not beings, just suppliers of dinner."*

What unpleasant scenarios, to be solely on the menu. "But here you are, talking to us," said Kiki.

*"And what fun it is! Others, my cousins, are gaining an interest in us. I wonder where this may go. Imagine you having conversations with your cows, your chickens, or your pigs. It would make for a lot more vegetarians, I am sure. What happens if you start to talk to your plants? Hmmmm. Okay, I must go. Heed my words."*

Nick and Kiki silently stared at the distant mountains.

"I'll stay in contact with Ramón. We'll come up with some path out of this mess," said Nick.

"I hate this," spat Kiki. "The thought of ripping another man's mind apart, no matter how evil he seems, is tearing at my soul. And our own government is two-timing us."

"It's not our government, but a few individuals."

Yeah, Kiki thought, but what is our government but a group of individuals.

"K, we cannot give them an excuse to separate us. It would seriously complicate any escape. Let's go finish with Andros."

# Chapter 47

The boat was a seventy-five foot luxury yacht with a crew of six. It had been fitted with all the instrumentation and communications gear needed to maintain contact, and to evade Coast Guard patrols. The Caribbean weather in late August was beautiful. Under other circumstances, it would have been a pure joy.

Their stateroom was luxurious, with teak paneling and polished brass fittings. The king-sized bed was gimbaled, remaining steady in turbulent seas. Whoever owned this yacht before liked mirrors.

Along with the boat ride came Zyra, a tall wiry woman of few words. Her skin was the color of ebony. Intense black eyes shone from a face of angles and points framed with short black hair. She was their *assistant* and Dianne Coleman's agent. She radiated confidence. Nick suspected that under her baggy coveralls she was lean and tough. They must be cautious around her.

Nothing eluded her eyes as they set up the isolation chamber in another stateroom. It was also gimbaled to minimize motion. They had very little contact with the captain or crew.

The first night at sea, Kiki pulled Nick aside while they were alone on the upper deck. "Nick, that woman, Zyra, worries me. She's strange, intense. I can't get any reading on her."

"She's Coleman's spy, acting as her agent on site. She's also our replacement once she thinks she can take over interrogations."

Kiki put her hand on Nick's arm. "Nick, I've seen you work. You have a talent for keeping our targets on the edge. Between the drug balance, the isolation chamber, and your questioning, they completely displace from reality. You make them want to tell us everything."

"Thanks for that vote of confidence. The sooner Zyra can take over, the sooner we can get out of this."

"I don't believe they're going to let us out," she lamented. Her head moved from side to side. They knew too much to be turned loose.

Two days out of port, the boat slowed. The clatter of a helicopter announced the arrival of their next victim. Kiki and Nick went to the helipad, ducked under the spinning rotors, and opened the door. Two men dressed in black hopped out and unloaded the unconscious man strapped to a gurney. Another figure sat in the shadows of the chopper bay. The two men wheeled and carried the gurney into the stateroom.

"Strip him and put him in the vat," Nick instructed. They spoke not a word but complied.

"I will interpret," stated Zyra.

Why did they need an interpreter? wondered Kiki. Nick spoke Arabic fluently.

"And watch us," said Kiki.

The woman nodded. "Of course, that too."

Once the bearded man was in the vat, the men glanced at the chamber and left. Zyra looked at Nick and Kiki, then at the nude form in the vat. Her gaze never left Nick as he attached the monitors and inserted the IVs. Once the soft restraints were attached, Nick filled the chamber with brine. The soft whine of the circulating pump was almost unheard as he closed the lid. The monitors on the wall showed the vital signs of the man in the chamber.

Nick watched Zyra study every move. "You sedated him heavily. We'll have to wait a while to bring him around," he said to her.

"Who is he?" asked Kiki.

"His name is Kedar," answered Zyra. "He is working with Los Christos as the World Under Islam man, the jihadists behind this campaign."

Her forthcoming attitude troubled Kiki. She had expected a reply like, "You do not need to know." Usually information was closely guarded. Her accent was not familiar.

"Mohammed mentioned him during interrogation," said Nick. "Let's get some coffee. Once we start, it could be a long session."

On deck, Nick looked at the blue waters of the Caribbean. They had left Pensacola in the dead of night. He knew enough navigation to tell they were sailing south-southwest. That route and their leisurely speed would take them near Cancún in a couple of days or so. They stayed out of sight of land. He suspected they would remain outside the twenty-five mile limit of Mexican control.

The helicopter was almost too big for the pad on the fantail of the boat. New and modern, it had no markings. Nobody would be able to identify it. Two men lounged around it. Pilot and copilot, Nick thought. They had that look. The other two men had disappeared.

"You guys want coffee?" he called to them. That got him a sharp look from Zyra. They nodded, and the group made their way to the shaded tables. There was no one to serve them, so each grabbed a cup, filled it at the urn and sat.

"Mike," said the tall sandy haired one Nick pegged as the pilot. They shook hands. "Good coffee," he said.

"Nick," he said holding out his hand to the shorter dark haired man.

"Steve." He shook Nick's hand.

"Kiki, Zyra," Nick said pointing at each of them. The men eyed the two women.

Kiki knew she was being rated. She liked it. Zyra ignored them.

"Flying long?" Nick asked.

"Three stints in the Middle East," said Mike. "You fly?"

"Nah, only a passenger," said Nick.

Steve's gaze turned to Kiki. "Kiki is not a common name. We heard of a sniper in the Sandbox named Kiki. You ever hear of her?"

Zyra's eyes hardened.

"Nope. I'm from Arizona. Never been overseas," said Kiki. "Got a job here as a nurse. Not bad duty. I'm working on my tan."

The men laughed. Nick saw Zyra relax, but only a little.

"Gorgeous weather," said Kiki.

"It is now," said Mike. "We've been watching a depression in the Atlantic eight-hundred miles east. Nothing to worry about for a few days."

They chitchatted a while longer, carefully staying away from any mention of the passenger.

"How about showing me your chopper? What is it?"

Mike and Steve both smiled. "It's a Sikorsky S-76. Newer model," said Steve. Chopper pilots loved to show off their ride. The three strolled to the helicopter.

"It is not a good idea to talk with others," said Zyra.

"It would seem strange if we didn't," explained Kiki. "It would raise more questions in their minds, make them more attentive."

Zyra nodded once. They watched as Nick entered the helicopter. Through the windshield, they could see Mike pointing out features. Nick nodded, placing his hands on the controls, his head swiveling as he looked at various gages. He waved at Kiki, a big grin on his face.

After twenty minutes, they returned to the table.

"Time to get back to our patient," said Nick. Zyra and Kiki stood, and the three headed below deck.

Nick was aware of Zyra's scrutiny as he checked monitors and adjusted drips. Kiki watched Zyra watching Nick like a specimen.

"We're ready," announced Nick.

Zyra went to the monitor and link. Within minutes a view of Freddy and Dianne appeared.

# Chapter 48

Under Zyra's watchful eye, Nick slowly increased the stimulant drip, his attention glued to the monitors. As heart rate and respiration increased, brainwave activity showed Kedar was waking up.

"Where am I?" Kedar asked in Arabic. Nick let Zyra interpret. "Hello?" Kedar's voice rang out.

Nick told Zyra to say nothing. She remained mute. Nick pointed to the monitors indicating heart rate, respiration, and brainwave activity increasing. Zyra took in everything.

"Allah, help me! Where am I?" cried Kedar.

Nick handed Zyra the script. She pressed the microphone button and spoke.

*"You are with me, Kedar. I am your God."*

"Why can I feel nothing? Why can I see nothing? Why is your voice in my head?"

*"You have no need of the senses of your body here. You have left that world behind. You must prepare to enter Paradise. You must sing the song of your life. Start with your last memories,"* Zyra said.

"I was in the compound of Los Christos when an explosion blew in the gate, killing the guards, stunning me. Men in black masks surrounded me. One raised a gun. It was the last image I have. Am I dead?"

*"You are,"* Zyra stated. *"Continue with the song of your life. Leave nothing out. Those awaiting you must know of your deeds."*

Thus began the interrogation of Kedar with Zyra reading from the script Nick had written. At times, he would give her specific questions to ask, guiding Kedar through his life, eliciting information. She soon learned the phraseology needed, and Kedar spun out his story. It went on for hours before Nick pointed to the monitors and signaled Zyra it was time for a break. He put Kedar back to sleep.

The next day was a repeat. Zyra now knew the questioning routine. They finished late that afternoon.

***

Dianne Coleman's face filled the monitor. She smiled. "The details about Kandahar will give us what we need to go after the hierarchy of The World Under Islam," said Dianne. "I'll put eyes over that area today. Good job, Zyra, Nick, Katherine."

It was the first time Kiki had seen her smile. "What do we do with him now?" she asked.

The smile disappeared. "He'll be loaded back on the chopper," said Dianne, in an airy voice.

"And then?" asked Nick.

The view changed to Freddy. "We'll take care of him." Her smile seemed genuine, unlike Dianne's. "Nothing for you to worry about. Just relax and take it easy tomorrow."

Everybody was happy, time to test the waters, and get some plans moving. "Can I get phone access?" asked Nick. "I'd like to check on a few things."

"What things?" asked Dianne sharply.

"My bank account," said Nick. And a few other things he thought.

"Yeah, okay," said Freddy. "Talk to you in a couple days."

"One call to the Caymans," said Dianne. She had to keep them on a short leash.

Nick turned from the monitor to the isolation chamber, careful to keep his face expressionless. Zyra watched as he changed the drips, putting Kedar under again.

"If he's conscious when we open the chamber," explained Nick, "he'll realize he isn't dead. His mind will snap, he may get violent."

Zyra just stared at him, her face a mask, her eyes dead.

When the monitors showed the regular respiration and slow heartbeat he wanted, Nick drained the chamber. Somehow, Kedar looked smaller than when they had put him in the chamber, as if he'd lost something. Nick detached IVs and the sensor pads. Zyra left.

She returned with the two men who had brought him in. They lifted the unconscious figure out, wrapped him in a robe, and placed him on a gurney. The boat slowed. Minutes later, the whine of the helicopter starting could be heard. Zyra oversaw the men as they climbed aboard the chopper and secured the stretcher. She watched Nick and Kiki wave as the helo lifted off. She did not wave.

"I wonder if he will even make it to land," said Kiki.


Back in their stateroom, Nick placed the call to Kings Town in the Caymans. Aware that there was certainly a bug in their stateroom and a tap on the phone, he spoke into the telephone handset. "Ramón, this is Nick. How are you?"

"Mr. Nick! I am fine," came back the rich basso voice. "How are you?"

"Kiki and I are doing well. We wanted to check with you about our bank balance."

"Ah, Mr. Nick, it keeps growing. You have a wonderful employer. He pays on time."

"Ramón , have you found any houses like we talked of before?"

There was a pause. "Yes, yes I have some for you to consider. They are all beautiful, but one, it is special and in the price range you gave me."

"Ramón, we trust you completely. Make the deal, with a good commission for yourself. Retain any staff needed to keep it up. Kiki and I will come soon for a visit. I will let you know the dates."

"Thank you, Mr. Nick. I am looking forward to your visit."

Freddy Foster pushed back from her desk and looked at Dianne Coleman. "Sounds like our interrogators are planning to retire soon," she said.

Flicking imaginary lint from her black suit, Dianne sneered, "I don't care what their plans are.

We're going to keep them working. Zyra needs more training. As soon as we get Julio Cardenas in that chamber and milk him dry about Los Christos, I'm sending that boat to the Middle East."

"Dianne, they've done everything we asked." Freddy didn't like where this was going.

"Freddy, we need them. And they need to learn who's in charge." She stood to leave. A smile crossed her face. "I'm going out to that boat to watch them question Señor Cardenas. I want a first-hand look at this interrogation, and I need to get things moving on the next phase."

Freddy looked at her. It was unexpected and a bad idea. They needed to maintain distance from this. She shook her head. This wasn't right, but she said nothing.

# Chapter 49

The captain and Zyra approached Nick and Kiki's table as they ate an early dinner. His uniform was immaculately white, his hat firmly on his head. On his thin face, he wore a concerned expression. Zyra's face was expressionless.

"We may have a situation developing you could help with. Our radar has picked up two small craft heading toward us. These waters have reported pirate attacks. I was second in command on a freighter in the Indian Ocean, and this looks like a couple of pirate craft heading our way. I know your background," he said looking at Kiki. "Could you stand by if we need it?"

"Dianne Coleman took my bag of toys away when we boarded," said Kiki.

"I will return them to you," said Zyra. "You pick the best vantage point. I will bring them to you."

Kiki looked up at her. "I'll be in my cabin getting a few things. Please bring the bag there."

She looked at the captain. "Also, we'll need a good pair of night vision binoculars. We'll be on the upper deck. I will need their range and heading from your radar."

"Yes, ma'am."

"I will be your spotter," stated Zyra, no room for argument in her voice.

Nick frowned, starting to object. He didn't like being separated from Kiki, even while on the boat, but this wasn't a battle to fight. "I'll be on the bridge and call out the information to you."

Zyra watched as Kiki chose the Remington model 700. These guys probably had Rocket Propelled Grenade anti-tank weapons; she had to take them out before they got into range. Quickly, Kiki assembled the rifle, carefully fitting the night vision scope and the sling. Zyra nodded at her choice.

"Why don't you do this?" asked Kiki.

Zyra turned cold eyes on Kiki. "I prefer my enemies close. I am better when I see their eyes." Her smile chilled Kiki.

She handed Zyra the box of 7.62 X 51 match ammo. They headed for the top deck, donning intercom headsets.

"K, the two craft are 2000 meters out at two-o'clock. It looks like they are splitting up to approach us from both port and starboard."

"Thanks, Nick." His voice was reassuring. She swung her rifle in the direction Nick had given.

From their perch, they had a great view. Within seconds, Kiki spotted the two Zodiacs through the scope on her rifle. She tracked their progress across the sea, the crosshairs moving from one to the other.

"Captain, in the lead boat I see three people – one is steering, one is holding a rifle, and the third has an RPG," Kiki called to the intercom.

"It is the same for the following boat," said Zyra, using the binoculars.

"The captain is logging everything, K. We have to have a record, so keep giving us information as you see it."

"The boats cannot be allowed closer than 500 meters – the maximum range for the RPGs," stated Zyra.

Kiki settled into the all-business mode of a top sniper. "If they're heading our way at 1000 meters, I'm taking out the guys with the RPGs, the boat on the starboard side first. This late in the day, he could get the sun behind him, making for a difficult shot. Our boat is stable, but they're bouncing around. This could be tough."

"Captain," Zyra called to the intercom, "keep track of the port boat. We focus on the starboard one first. We are clear to fire?"

The captain's voice came over the intercom, "We've tried to reach them on all hailing channels. No response. If they continue toward us, you're cleared."

"Nick, sing out when the starboard boat is 1000 meters range," said Kiki, her voice cool and flat.

Kiki and Zyra watched the boat swing on an intercept course and accelerate. At the call from the Nick, she put the crosshairs on the RPG man. Timing carefully, she fired. The rifle bucked against her shoulder in a familiar punch.

"Hit," called Zyra, her voice hard.

Through the scope, Kiki watched the man fly backwards overboard still clutching the RPG. The boat immediately slowed and turned. They would not have heard the shot over the sound of the outboard, probably suspecting he lost his balance and fell.

"Zyra," she commanded, "watch that boat. Nick, where's the portside boat?"

"He's at ten-o'clock, 900 meters."

"Got him," said Kiki. "He's starting a run toward us." Again, she targeted the RPG man and fired.

"Low by one meter, in front by one meter," called Zyra.

"Shit," Kiki yelled. She jacked another round into the chamber, centered the crosshairs, let out a breath, and squeezed the trigger.

"Hit," called Zyra.

This shot struck the man in the abdomen. He doubled over, dropping the RPG. Kiki fired another round into the outboard. The boat stopped.

"How's the first boat doing?" she asked Nick.

"He seems to be stopped."

In a quiet voice, Zyra spoke. "They are idling and have pulled the body into the boat. They are pointing at us."

Kiki fired a round into the outboard. The boat sat still in the water.

"Boats are disabled. What do you want me to do, Captain?"

"Kill them all," said Zyra, as if talking about insects.

Kiki paused. She put a round into the inflatable chambers in the front of each boat. Looking up from her rifle, she stared at the unemotional face of Zyra. "We'll leave them alone. They may get help before they sink."

Nick's voice interrupted the stares between the two women. "We're calling in an attempted pirate attack with the location to the Coast Guard. With any luck, our military will pick them up."

"Or not," shrugged Zyra.

"Nice shooting, K."

"Yeah, like old times," she responded, but it wasn't. In the Sandbox, she would have killed them all.

"You would leave a viper alive?" asked Zyra, her thin eyebrows rose.

Something was different within Kiki now.

# Chapter 50

Nick and Katherine returned to the stateroom to clean the isolation chamber. Sitting in the chairs, they looked at each other. "What's next?" wondered Kiki aloud.

Nick glanced at the satellite monitor. It was a bug, set up to listen even when it didn't indicate it was connected. "We wait for the next victim." Nick grimaced.

**"Katherine, Nick, you know what's coming, correct? Dianne Coleman really does hate you. You are a couple, a relationship she has never enjoyed. You represent a threat to her power base. Her fear of that, her hate for you, and her drive for power will make for a delicious meal."**

Nick looked at Kiki. They rose, walking away from the monitor and out of the stateroom. "Why are you helping us?" muttered Nick.

**"You have controlled your hatred and fear and are not my choice of flavors**

*anymore. You are a welcome change for me from the dull conversations with the others of me. I like you."*

"And we still cause fear and hatred in other people," stated Kiki.

*"You continue to do that for me. Thank you. I have given Dianne a little tweak. I think you will find it interesting. I know I will enjoy it."*

"What about Zyra? She radiates danger to us. I feel it," said Kiki.

*"You must be cautious of her. She is like an empty plate at the dinner table for me. If she were to kill you, her only emotion would be remorse at not picking your brains dry first. She would feel satisfaction, like swatting a mosquito, no sorrow. Her mind is unclouded by emotions so tightly controlled nothing comes out. Heed my warning about Dianne Coleman. Zyra answers to her*

***only. When Dianne Coleman feels Zyra can take over, you will be in danger."***

No sound had been uttered. The Presence spoke in their heads. They returned to their stateroom. Soundlessly, they went to bed, clinging to each other in the dark. Their lovemaking began tentatively, each aware it might be the last time. Once started, it grew in intensity, despite the monitors, or maybe because of them. Sleep came slowly as storms of questions raged within them. They had only each other as their anchors.

Morning brought no new solutions. "Let's go up on deck and enjoy the sunrise," said Nick.

To the east they saw red clouds, signaling a change in the weather. It must be the tropical depression the chopper pilot had told them about. Heading south, there was a good chance they would miss it.

The distant clatter of the helicopter grew louder, signaling that the peaceful day of ease was over. They had spent much of it together in their stateroom. The boat slowed. It had only been one day off, but a welcome relief. As the chopper settled, Nick and Kiki went below deck to ready the isolation chamber for the next victim.

Within minutes, Zyra and Steve carried in a stretcher. Strapped to it was a slight man with dark skin and black hair.

"Strip him and put him into the chamber," Nick ordered. The two complied without a word. Nick went about the preparations. Zyra watched Nick as he made the man ready.

Once the unconscious man was in the chamber, Nick attached the sensor pads and inserted the IV, watching the monitors to be sure everything was working well. He closed the chamber, and glanced at Steve as he left.

Zyra hovered. "We can begin soon?"
Nick nodded.


Dianne Coleman entered the bridge of the ship. Her heels clicked on the floor, her stride and black suit spoke of power. "Captain, change course. Head east. We're going to Guantanamo. "

"Ma'am, there's a tropical depression building to the east of us. It will reach hurricane force within the next twelve hours. I am considering sheltering at Cozumel."

She brushed her lapel and turned an icy gaze on the man. "Captain, you can make Guantanamo. You'll shelter and fuel there. After the storm passes, you're heading to the Mediterranean."

He shook his head. "With all due respect, ma'am, we'd have to run at full power to make Cuba before this storm hits. Even then, we'll be in rough seas. If that storm changes course, we'll be in the middle of it."

Dianne Coleman stared daggers at him. How dare he defy her! "If you ever want another job as captain of anything more than a rowboat, you'll get moving. I'm going below."

***

In the stateroom, Kiki and Nick felt the ship change course. She looked a question at him. What was going on?

Without knocking, Dianne entered. Kiki drew a sharp breath. How did she get here?

"Hi, Katherine. Hello, Nick." Dianne nodded at Zyra, who nodded back. "I thought I'd sit in on a session for myself, at least for a while."

Kiki felt the deck rumble as the engines revved. "Are we changing course, speeding up?"

"There's a storm coming, so the captain's moving to shelter," answered Dianne.

Nick shook his head. "This rumble and increased movement might be felt in the chamber. I'm not sure if he," Nick nodded at the black

312

coffin-like box, "will feel it. If he does, it will throw off the session. Who is he?"

"He's Julio Cardenas, the head of the Los Christos cartel. We're gathering information for Freddy and the Mexican government."

Nick and Kiki exchanged quick glances. The virus had warned them. This wasn't right. Nick knew they should be heading south-southwest to seek shelter from the storm. They had turned to port – east.

Nick looked at Dianne. "It will be a while until we can begin. He's too heavily sedated right now." Nick needed time to think.

"How long?" asked Dianne.

"An hour at the most," said Nick.

"Let's go up on deck," said Kiki. "I need some air. There's nothing to do here."

On deck, Nick asked Dianne, "Coffee?" She took the cup from him and walked to the urn, helping herself.

Kiki leaned close to Nick. "Nick, something's wrong." she whispered.

"I know." They walked toward the railing, away from Dianne and Zyra. "We're heading east, toward the storm. I think we're going to have to make our escape at the first opportunity."

"How?"

Nick saw the troubled look in her eyes. He nodded at the helicopter.

At the coffee pot, Zyra put a hand on Dianne's arm. "Ma'am, will you be staying?"

"Don't worry. I have no doubt of your capability," answered Dianne. "We're moving into the Middle East. I had to get things underway."

Zyra's eyebrows rose.

"After the interrogation of Cardenas, we will have wrapped up the Mexican operation. All that's left is mopping up the cartel. Cardenas will give us the information the government needs for that," said Dianne. "We're required in Afghanistan."

"You are going with us?" Zyra asked. Her eyebrows raised in a rare expression on her normally frozen face.

"No, I'll only be here a few hours. Once we get Cardenas going, I'll fly back. I'll stay in the stateroom with Nick and Katherine. You will stay with the captain to be sure he follows my orders. Under no circumstances let him change course. Lock the door to prevent interference. I'll call you when I need you."

The wind freshened, coming over the port side. Nick approached Dianne. Her hair whipped around her face.

"We're heading east," said Nick, nodding forward. "That's into the storm."

"We're going to Guantanamo. We have other candidates for interrogation there. We can make it before the storm hits. It's a safe haven." She turned away, signaling an end to Nick's questions.

Kiki looked ahead. The blue water was turning gray. Waves were coming out of the north, giving the boat a roll.

Nick went to the chopper where Mike and Steve huddled inside.

"Why don't you guys use our stateroom and get out of this weather. We'll come get you when Ms. Coleman is ready to leave."

They nodded their thanks and headed below.

"Let's go back," Nick said to Dianne. "Our new candidate should be ready."

They rose. Zyra headed for the bridge. Nick and Kiki exchanged glances.

# Chapter 51

Dianne closed the door to the stateroom and turned to gaze at the isolation chamber.

"Where's Zyra?" asked Kiki.

"She's doing another task for me. It's not your concern." She walked toward the chamber, placing her hand on it. "I'll be with you for a while today," she said with a smile, chilling Kiki.

Kiki activated the link connections. Freddy appeared on the monitor.

"Dianne, I see you made it," she said. "Any problems?"

"None. We have Julio ready for questioning."

Nick spoke up. "Freddy, are you onboard with this?"

"You mean questioning Cardenas?"

"That too, but you know what I'm talking about."

A smile crept onto Dianne's face. "Nick, Kiki, whatever are you referring to? We're going to question Cardenas while we travel to Guantanamo. We have prisoners there we must interrogate."

Sure, thought Nick. Far too many prisoner advocates and attorneys were at Gitmo for them to fly under the radar. Disappearing prisoners would not work. It was a way-stop to elsewhere. Nick and Kiki stared mutely at the monitor. Freddy said nothing.

"Let's get started," said Dianne, clapping her hands and turning toward the chamber.

Nick nodded to Kiki. She touched the off-button on the link. Nick took Dianne by surprise, the hypodermic sinking into her neck.

Her hand flew to her neck. "What the hell did you do," she screamed. "What was that?" She stepped toward Nick, one hand fumbling for her purse.

Kiki locked the door. Nick caught Dianne's slumping form. Kiki reconnected the link, but not the camera.

"Nick, Kiki, I've lost your signal," came Freddy's voice.

"We're having a bit of trouble here, Freddy We'll have it taken care of in a minute," said Kiki.

Nick opened the chamber, disconnected Julio, and pulled him out. He stripped Dianne and hooked her up. She was in the chamber within minutes. Glancing at her, he went to the monitors, checked them. He started the drips, with a last look at her as the brine circulated in the chamber. Now, see how you like it, sweetheart, he thought. He closed the black lid with a satisfying click.

Kiki hit the mute button on the link and went to the intercom. "Captain, we need a slowdown. Ms. Coleman is going to depart in a few minutes."

"Aye."

Nick wrapped Julio in a large towel and threw him over his shoulder in a fireman's carry. Kiki opened the door and checked to see that the corridor was clear. She stepped back and nodded at Nick, who headed aft and up to the chopper pad.

Kiki pulled the .380 automatic from Dianne's purse. She grabbed several tote-bags from a corner and bundled Dianne's clothes into one. At their stateroom, she locked the door. By the time she got to the chopper, Nick had strapped Julio down. Kiki climbed into the Sikorsky S-76's cargo door.

"You know how to fly one of these things?" asked Kiki.

"You don't think I just rode during all my time in Afghanistan. I never got licensed, but I did a lot of flying," said Nick, as the rotors spun up.

As the turbines whined, the pilots came running out. Alerted by the sound, they had smashed through the stateroom door.

"Mike, Steve, we're going to take a little ride in your chopper with Ms. Coleman," Nick said, nodding toward the back.

Both pilots glanced at the bundled figure strapped to the gurney.

Kiki pointed the gun at them. "Without you, sorry."

Their mouths fell open. Steve started to speak, but Kiki waved the gun for emphasis. They moved back from the pad, hands raised. The boat was rising with the swells, but not badly enough to prevent takeoff.

She closed the door and moved toward the co-pilot's seat. Nick lifted off and turned west, staying low to the water. He wobbled the copter to appear like an unsure pilot. They might think he crashed.

"K, I need you to put latitude nineteen point three zero and longitude minus eighty-one point three six into the Flight Management System."

"Where's that?"

"Kings Town airport in the Caymans. We won't land there, but close to it." Nick picked up the microphone. Within minutes, he had Ramón on the line.

"Nick, my friend. Are you coming for a visit?" His deep basso voice seemed to contain a smile.

"We are. Is our house ready? We're arriving in a helicopter, but not at the airport."

Ramón began to laugh. "Mr. Nick, You are full of surprises. I'll pick you up at the Island Air Hangar. They'll think you are another tourist flight."

"Great, Ramón. We'll be there in two hours. We'd like to see the house immediately. Can you arrange for the staff to be there?"

"Certainly. It will be done."

Once the boat dipped below the horizon, Nick turned south and engaged the autopilot. With this tailwind, they should have no problems making Cayman.

Dianne Coleman floated up from unconsciousness into darkness. Slowly it dawned on her where she was. She tried to move, but was paralyzed. She held her panic down. It was nothing, just a warm bath. She could handle that. Someone would come for her. Soon. A niggling doubt wormed up within her.

*"Nick, Katherine, this is wonderful. Dianne is trying so hard to keep her fear under control, but as you know, it is only a matter of time. Being afraid of her fear is a tangy flavor. I like it. I have given her a little push. Panic is so tasty."*

From the bridge, Zyra, watched the chopper depart. She was glad to be out of Dianne's watchful eye. The woman reminded her of a snake.

"You may resume course, Captain. She has left," said Zyra.

The captain ordered the course change and full speed ahead. The boat rolled and surged forward toward the line of gray water ahead.

Steve and Mike pounded on the passageway door leading to the bridge, but no one answered. It had been locked by Zyra to prevent interference. She knew how to follow orders.

# Chapter 52

Nick located the small airport without a problem. He landed the helicopter on a remote pad away from the main hangar and shut it down. With the weather forecast, the touristy flights were postponed. The parking lot was empty, except for the black limousine.

Nick and Kiki greeted the huge black man with hugs.

"Mr. Nick, Miss Katherine. It is good to see you at last. So you are retiring from the business grind to our fair island?"

"It is not by choice," said Nick. "Unsavory characters would very much like to get their hands on us. We need to leave immediately."

"Ho, ho. So full of surprises. No worries, mon. Everything is set."

Nick nodded at the helicopter. "We have an unwilling passenger that we will need to take with us."

"Should I be surprised? No, I think not."

Nick secured Julio and gagged him. They loaded the unconscious man into the trunk of the car.

"The helicopter is yours, Ramón, but you need remove it quickly and alter it. People will come looking for it. Consider it payment for your service, present and future."

Ramón held the rear door of the limo open for them. "Thank you, Mr. Nick. I know just the client who needs such an aircraft. He will pay handsomely. By selling this to him, you boost my reputation."

At the marina, Ramón opened the limo door and pointed at the boats. One in particular stood out. "Ramón, this is a gorgeous vessel." Kiki looked at the sixty-five-foot trimaran, resembling *Star Trek's* Romulan bird of prey. "What size is the crew?"

He beamed at her. "Miss Katherine, it has a crew of five, but after you learn to sail, you can get by with two or three." He turned toward Nick. "Much of it is automated. It is outfitted with the latest electronics, navigation equipment, radar, sonar, satellite, everything you need to sail around the world. Come, let me show you the interior." Above them, the rigging rattled in the building wind.

***

Zyra braced herself against a bulkhead as the wind-driven waves from the north increased the roll as the boat drove east. "Hold your course, Captain," she admonished. She looked ahead at the whitecaps, mares tails starting to form in the building wind.

The captain frowned. "If this continues to build, we'll have to turn into it or face the possibility of capsizing. You do understand that?"

"How far away is Cuba?" Zyra asked.

"Less than an hour. We can tuck close to the island until we arrive at Guantanamo. It'll be on the lee side of the island, until the eye passes. By that time we should have secure anchorage."

The intercom crackled. "Captain, there is an emergency message from FBI agent Freddy Foster." The captain looked at Zyra. She nodded.

"Put it through," he said. "This is Captain Markel. Over."

"Captain, this is FBI Assistant Director Freddy Foster. We were in contact with Assistant Director Dianne Coleman of the CIA but were cut off. Is she there? Over."

"She flew out an hour ago. Have you tried to reach her helicopter? Over."

"We thought she was still on board. We'll try that. Can you check with Nick or Katherine to see if they know anything? Over."

"I'll send somebody now." He signaled his mate to go. Within seconds Mike and Steve rushed onto the bridge.

"That fucking guy stole our chopper!"

"What?" shouted Zyra. Her face reddened in rage. She spun, looking behind them toward the horizon.

"Yeah. They held us at gunpoint and stole our helicopter. I didn't even know the asshole could fly."

"They took Director Coleman with them?" asked Zyra.

"Yeah! yeah, I think so." Steve nodded. "She was wrapped and strapped to the gurney in the back, at least that's what they said. They headed west, low so radar wouldn't pick them up. I don't think the guy was a very good pilot. He yawed a lot on takeoff. That was over an hour ago."

"Director Foster, did you get that?" asked the Captain.

"Yeah, she's been kidnapped by those two. Where could they go?"

The captain thought for a moment. "If I were them, I'd swing around and head to Cancún. Once in Mexico, they could disappear. The only thing south is the Caymans. Those islands are easy to bottle up. They'd be trapped."

"Okay, we'll alert our people in Cancún. Where are you now?"

"We'll be in Cuban waters within an hour and at Guantanamo in two. It's a good thing, too. This storm is intensifying."

"We've been watching it too, Captain. It's now hurricane Gloria, a class one."

# Chapter 53

"Where to, Captain Nick?" asked the rail thin man. His hair was bleached white, his skin the texture of dark brown leather from the sun. Cutoff jeans hung from his hips, his arms protruded like toothpicks from his tie-dyed tee shirt.

Nick held Kiki and looked into her eyes. "What do you think?"

She walked across the cabin to the chart table. It was polished teak with a large flat-screen monitor. The push of a button, and it lit up with a map of the Caribbean. Kiki pointed to the red dot that was them on Cayman Island. She traced a path across the screen. "Let's head south, Cozumel then Aruba."

"You heard the lady, Rodolfo."

"Aye aye, Captain Nick."

They both turned to the mustached man in the easy chair. "Julio, what do you think of a trip to Cozumel?" asked Nick.

"Si´. Put me there." He smiled. "You save my life. If you ever need anything, money, help, anything at all, contact me. It is yours."

"Nick, will we ever be able to go home?" asked Kiki.

They heard the snap of the sails filling, felt the boat move beneath their feet. "Maybe we are home." Nick gave her a hug. They walked up on deck.

***"Enjoy yourselves. You created quite a feast for me. Another of me who likes the sweet tastes of love is now dining with you."***

"Another of you?" cried Kiki. "We will be forced to host another parasite?"

***"You wound me. I have not been that bad, have I? I helped you."***

"You did warn us," confirmed Nick. "But the idea we are feeding a being with no choice is hard to take."

***"It is why you are here. I learned to consider you as more than just food. You are too interesting to abandon. I will visit from time to time. Ta ta."***

Nick looked into Kiki's eyes. "At least we know about it. I'm not sure that is a plus."

She nodded. Feeling helpless didn't change anything but her attitude.

R. L. Clayton

# Epilogue

Freddy Foster stared out her picture window. It was a beautiful day, with brilliant sun and golden leaves as fall approached. The middle of a workday, and she was home – administrative leave. Her 'case' was under review. Al Bowers and Homeland Security had pulled out as soon as the domestic operations were over. The catastrophe with Nick and Kiki came to rest on her desk. She'd lost two operatives of immense value, a high level target, a senior CIA agent, and a new helicopter. No trace had been found. All ports within their range had been checked, coastlines searched. After three weeks, the sea searches had been scaled back yesterday. They could only assume the helicopter had crashed into the sea. Some jetsam had been found, but not conclusive of a crash. The transponder must be dead. No signal had been received. She'd be lucky to only be fired. They did shut down a major terrorist thrust in America. Right now, that did not seem to weigh heavily on the plus side of her balance sheet.

Freddy knew it was wrong to kidnap Nick and Kiki, imprisoning them and forcing them to continue the interrogations. The information was desperately needed, but these actions had gone badly awry. Freddy should have spoken up, opposed this program, but she didn't.

Dianne Coleman was under intense psychiatric care. It was three days before someone looked in the isolation chamber. She had moments of clarity, but they were only moments. Most of the time, she was comatose or babbling. Her prognosis was not good. Freddy shuddered when she thought about Dianne Coleman, lost but alive.

Making enemies of Nick and Kiki had been disastrous. Part of her was thankful they were dead. They were, weren't they?

She looked out the window again, with different eyes, searching for danger, perhaps death. A tremble of fear raced up her spine. She backed up and closed the curtains. Turning away, she cradled her head in her hands. Ahead of her loomed a life of looking over her shoulder, expecting death at any time. Was this the day, the minute, the second? A voice formed in her head.

**_"Yum. Hello, Freddy."_**

For and excerpt from the next book in the
Dead Series, please turn the page.

# DEAD

# RECKONING

## Descent into Dystopia

# Prologue

August 20

The Boeing 777 from Tokyo to Los Angeles had reached cruising altitude and the attendants were taking dinner orders. Anatoly Tsaryov watched his fellow passengers through slitted eyes, pretending to be asleep. The family in the five-by row across from him was trying to settle down, get the three kids in their seats.

"Mommy, I have to go to the bathroom," said the six-year-old girl. Her mom stood to let her pass into the aisle. The girl skipped down the aisle to the bathroom, her curls and pink dress bouncing in time.

Perfect, thought Anatoly. He withdrew a small pink bottle of Mr. Bubbles from his carryon. As the girl returned, he pulled out the wand and blew a stream of bubbles into the aisle. Her eyes got wide. "You want to blow some bubbles?"

She reached for the bottle, fingers flexing, then looked at her mom, her mouth open. He held out the bottle. Her mom nodded. Gingerly, she took it from him and blew a stream of bubbles into the air. They spread over the passengers near them, who began to laugh. The girl ran down the aisle, streams of bubbles in a cloud behind her.

Bubbles, yes. But much more, thought Anatoly. The solution contained the *variola major virus*, small pox, the virulent form. By the end of the flight, most of the passengers would be exposed. Anatoly wasn't the only international jet passenger carrying Mr. Bubbles bottles that day.

In the crowded immigration line, he gave a bottle to another child, a boy of five or six, who happily spread the bubbles over the laughing crowd, welcoming the diversion from customs. Airports in New York, Seattle, Atlanta, Dallas, Chicago and Washington, D.C. were all supposed to enjoy a bubble snowstorm.

The taxi dropped him off at his hotel. Crowds thronged the lobby, children's laughter drowning out the elevator music. While standing in line to check in, he watched an elevated monorail approach. He'd always wanted to visit Disneyland as a child, and now he was being paid to visit it.

The receptionist smiled. "How may I help you?"

"I have a reservation under the name of Tsaryov. T-S-A-R-Y-O-V."

"Ah, yes. Here you are. Welcome to the Disneyland Hotel, Mr. Tasryov." She smiled and glanced at her monitor. "I see we have a package for you. I'll have it delivered to your room."

His room was decorated with Disney characters. The view looked out toward the Magic Kingdom. The knock on his door interrupted his thoughts. It was his package. He tipped the bellboy and set the box on the desk. The packing slip listed *Samples, Mr. Bubbles.*

Humming to himself, he put six bottles in his pockets and headed for the monorail terminal. Time to go to work.